HENRY'S EMPIRE

TALES FROM THE NORTHERN FRONTIER

BOB BENNETT

Published in Australia by Sid Harta Books & Print Pty Ltd,
ABN: 34632585293
23 Stirling Crescent, Glen Waverley, Victoria 3150 Australia
Telephone: +61 3 9560 9920, Facsimile: +61 3 9545 1742
E-mail: author@sidharta.com.au

First published in Australia 2022
This edition published 2022
Copyright © Bob Bennett 2022
Cover design, typesetting: WorkingType (www.workingtype.com.au)

Bennett, Bob
Henry's Empire
ISBN: 978-1-925707-84-7

pp176

About the Author

Bob Bennett grew up in Henry territory ... in Cloncurry and in Ayr on the Burdekin. A journalist with some 50 years' experience, he worked on newspapers in Townsville, Brisbane and Hong Kong before providing media services to government and business organisations. He also studied at both James Cook and Queensland Universities.

Author's thanks

Firstly, I would like to thank those early authors' books and reports on which *Henry's Empire* has heavily relied. Henry himself kept such detailed records that bring the times and places to life. I also thank authors such as S.E. Pearson *The Prospector of Argylla*, Hudson Fysh, *Taming the North*, M. Bennett *Christison of Lammermoor*, George Phillips, *Ernest Henry* and others that were consulted.

I would also like to thank the many people who helped me find the material for the book; librarians in James Cook University, the John Oxley Library, Queensland State Archives, the Royal Queensland Historical Society and the Queensland Police Museum.

My thanks also to Sid Harta Publishers for providing the opportunity to publish and for their continuing support.

And a special thanks to Frank Henry, descendant of Ernest Henry for his advice based on an extensive knowledge of the family's history.

Author's Note

Henry's Empire is an historical novel. It is a story of the life and times of Ernest Henry, English adventurer, explorer, grazier and miner. His life, and those of others he knew, are chronicled in various records and publications. Henry's Empire brings together the story / stories of those people in 19th century Australia, particularly Queensland.

Thus, this book borrows from various sources to tell the tales of that time. It involves inclusion, interpretation and surmise providing an unorthodox approach to traditional biographical material. It gives voice to those who are not, strictly recorded but who, by their participation in events which are recorded, are able to contribute. Extensive research into records and the assistance of a considerable number of people have contributed to *Henry's Empire*.

Contents

Chapter 1

CAPTIVE

Kalkadoon Territory,
Northwest Queensland
1884

They were arguing among themselves. Would they kill him or not? All day long, and now into the night around the campfire, the warrior natives tried to decide. For them too, the decision could mean life or death.

Ernest Henry lay wounded nearby. Wounded by one of their tribe. The blood was still seeping from his back into which the spear had been driven.

The Kalkadoons knew that if they killed him, they could expect bloody reprisals from other white men. To help him get back to other white men, however, might mean the same horrendous end.

Even if they helped the wounded man, would the men on horses come with guns? Such things had happened before. Would it not be better, some argued, to kill him and dispose of the body in the mountains where white man feared to come? The whites would not know what had happened. They might think he had had an accident or lost his way and perished.

Others pointed out that Henry, accident or not, made a habit of surviving. And he, of all men, could find his way anywhere.

Henry, already weakened by the wound, could only wait. And try to stay awake.

Chapter 2

A FAMILY OF FORTUNE

'The real purpose of empire,' Henry had heard it said, 'was to further enrich the rich.'

Yes, well, partly true, he thought.

There was also adventure and empire offered that in abundance. And opportunity. Even some felons, transported to far-away places like Australia, had become rich men and women with their own properties. Those opportunities were far less frequent in the home country even for members of the gentry.

And adventure was almost second nature to the Henry family.

Ernest was the second oldest in a family of four brothers. James, his oldest brother, had taken up tea planting in India. His cousin, Robert Gray, had been involved in active service. Robert's regiment in India took part in the second Relief of Lucknow during the Indian mutiny. Robert's brother, Charles, had been engaged in running the blockade in the War of Separation between the Northern and Southern States of America.

There was also his grandparents' experience in the West Indies where they were involved in sugar plantations. Henry warmed to his grandmother's stories of those times.

With a lifetime abroad in mind, Ernest enrolled as a naval cadet at the Portsmouth Navigation School. The skills he learned there were to assist him, much later, with his exploration of territories in what was to become Queensland.

His first venture was to Australia on the mail ship, *Victoria*. But his naval career was interrupted by another adventure possibility ... the Crimean War.

Henry's father, a former captain in the British army, bought Ernest a commission in the 72nd Highlanders Scottish Regiment and Ernest shipped to the battlefront ... only to arrive as the war ended.

Realising there was little opportunity for a soldier in a time of peace, Henry left the army and, with the backing of his family, sailed once more for Australia.

Chapter 3

PROGRESS REPORTS

(Author's note: Ernest Henry was an inveterate writer of letters and reports which have helped to tell his story)

VESSEL RED JACKET

7 DECEMBER 1857

My dear Father,

I begin a letter to you at so early a date, in the hope that we may pass some vessels during the calm weather, which we expect at this part of our voyage that will carry letters home. We are within a few days sail of the line. Our voyage has as yet been most prosperous. We experienced about four days rough weather at first, starting in the Channel, and two days of very light wind subsequently. Otherwise, we have done very well. She has run as many as fifteen and sixteen knots an hour, but the winds are lighter now, and are gradually decreasing, so we stand a good chance of being becalmed for a day or two about the line, so if we meet any vessel homeward bound at that time, we shall be able to send our letters. The *Red Jacket* is a good vessel in every respect. We have passed several others on the same course. She is very comfortable, and we live very well. I am just getting reconciled to the confinement.

Many people don't mind it, but I feel much like a bird in a cage. I have devoured no end of books. We have had beautiful weather. I seldom turn in before twelve at night or one in the morning. It is most delicious at night. The stars shine so bright, and there is generally a mild, gentle wind blowing. I lie on the deck looking at the stars, sometimes building castles as high, but my thoughts are generally with you at home.

I am very happy now, full of spirits of home. There are many very pleasant people on board. We certainly did not see the best of them as we came on board, some of them have been out before. I have obtained every kind of information from them. On the other hand, there are some very curious fish. The Captain is a very pleasant man and so is the doctor.

8 December 1857

This is the first wet day we have had since we were well out at sea. Nearly everybody is writing letters. We have overtaken three vessels today. One of them was an American whaler. The latter sent a boat to us with New York papers.

10 December 1857

We hardly made any way yesterday or this morning, but a breeze sprang up while we were at dinner, and there is a vessel homeward bound in sight, in which we hope to send our letters, but I am half afraid we shall not be able to, as it is raining cats and dogs.

Melbourne
7 February 1858
Hockin's Hotel

My dear Mother,

We were unable to send our letters by any ship. We have made a splendid run. Sighted Cape Otway (where they count the passage to) on January 28th at 5 am making sixty-eight days from Liverpool and sixty-three from land to land. (We were nearly five days in the Channel). We got inside the heads the following day but had not wind to carry us up to Melbourne, so were obliged to anchor for the night. We were favoured with a fair breeze the next day (Saturday) and were ashore in the afternoon, after seventy days on board. You will be glad, and I dare say surprised to hear that I never passed so pleasant a voyage. There were some of the best fellows I ever met on board. The only mishap we had which turned out all right in the end, was this, as we were coming into the Heads (we were two or three miles from land), we struck against the wreck of a vessel. The Captain fancied at first that we had grounded, and let go one of our anchors, the cable of which was afterwards cut, and we got off all right. I can't tell whether there was any danger, but some of the passengers were terribly frightened. We brought out the latest news and beat numbers of vessels that sailed before us. There was the *Chancellor* that sailed just a month before us, came in the day after us. We passed the Cape three days before her.

There was a young Irishman from Cork of the name of Gould, he has a brother in Hobarttown, and is a very gentlemanly man. Then we have Forwood and Danson, both come out for their health, both from Liverpool, and both gentlemen, and now you have my particular friends, all except one, who is my best, and in my opinion the best fellow on board. Papa will remember him, so I will with your leave, my dearest mother, write to him for a bit.

My dear Father,

You will remember when we were standing on board the *Red Jacket,* your pointing out to me a tall man with large whiskers and beard. You said you thought you had met him before. His name turned out to be Cannon. He has come out with the same ideas as I have, and we have arranged to see the country together. We must wait here for the mail which is not here yet (although due on the fifth of this month). As soon as it comes in, we are off. Cannon has a brother here in business. He is living in the same house with him now at St Kilda to which place you can get by rail in seven minutes. It is a pretty place with delightful sea-bathing. The first few days after we landed it rained in torrents. Most of the streets in Melbourne slope down from east to west, cutting others at right angles. The centre street is at the foot of either hill, and in wet weather it is flooded to an enormous extent. The ditches on either side are very deep, with small iron and wooden bridges over them to enable people to cross in wet weather. I was out one night at about 10 o'clock and it was all I could do to jump across the watercourse. They swelled so much during the night that a horse got in one of them and was drowned. People were taken across in cars.

The cars here are something like the Irish cars, the difference being that you face and back the horse. Most of them have awnings over them. They drive very fast.

NEW BATH HOTEL, ST. KILDA,

SATURDAY 13 FEBRUARY 1858

I came down here on Tuesday last. It is a much pleasanter place than Melbourne to stay at. The mail has not arrived yet and the home mail leaves on the fifteenth instant ... As soon as the mail does come in, Cannon and I start for the country. We propose going to Ballarat first. (The letter Mr Beck gave me is to a settler near there). It is about 78 miles from Melbourne. We can get there by coach. Horses we find would be a great deal too expensive. In fact, it will be bad enough without them. Of course, we shall be guided by circumstances as to our route after we have been to Ballarat, but our idea is to go as far as the Murray River. Dr Myer's brother is near Albury on the Murray or Hume River as that part of it seems to be called. We should be able to get there easily as it is on the high road to Sydney, 230 miles from Melbourne. We did think of going on to Sydney across country, but we are told

9

it would be much the best way to return to Melbourne and take the steamer. I should not go to Sydney as soon, but I called on the Dean[1] the other day (to whom I had a letter from Mr Gardiner), and he had one of his sons staying with him who has a station in this district, and he said he would strongly advise me not to settle on this side of the Murray, as Government was taking up a great deal of the land. I have heard a good deal said about Moreton Bay. Of course, it is impossible for me to say where I shall be when your answer reaches the Colony, but if our present intentions are carried out (with God's blessing) I shall be at Sydney or on my way there, so direct there. Now it strikes me very forcibly that is possible I may be getting hard up by that time. I don't think I shall be, for Cannon is as anxious to do it cheap as I am, but still it's quite possible, so if you were to send me some money to Sydney, it will keep me from working till I find out the best place ...

Sunday, February 14th...

Cannon went out to Canada to look at the place before he came here. A great many people seem to be emigrating from Canada to this place ... I think the life out here will suit me uncommonly well. You are so free and independent. You may go where you like and do what you will and say 'nothing to nobody' and 'nobody say nothing to you' as they say. But you must not think that I am going to waste my time. Now that I am out here, I mean downright work and nothing else.

---

1   [His family solicitor ^Dean McCartney]

COLAC, SUNDAY 28 FEBRUARY 1858

My dear Father,

We left Melbourne on Wednesday, February 24th ... We started at two-thirty in the Geelong boat, where we arrived at seven-thirty. We slept there that night and the next and left Geelong on Friday the 26th for Mr Manifold's station, near Timboon and Camperdown, about 75 miles from Geelong, almost due west. Mr Manifold is a friend of Cannon's. He is one of the largest cattle-owners in the country. We walked 25 miles the first day and the same the second, which brought us to this place. We rest here today (Sunday) and shall have 25 miles more to walk on Monday. I walk in these thick boots I had made in London. They are very comfortable. My feet would be burnt up in thin boots, the sun is so powerful. The greater part of our walk yesterday was across a large plain. For 15 miles we did not pass a tree or any habitation. It was very thirsty work. We got some tea at the first shepherd's hut we came to. It is the usual drink here at all hours of the day.

ROKEWOOD, TUESDAY 9 MARCH 1858

It is ten days since I began this letter in Colac. The night before we started for Mr Manifold's station, we had some bread and met put up in the evening, and a bottle of tea, as we intended to start as soon as it was light. The tea was put too hot in the bottle and burst during the night, so we were obliged to take our breakfast such as it was with brandy and water which we had in our flasks.

11

We started at five-thirty and had a very pleasant forest walk. Saw numbers of parrots of all sorts and sizes among others the King parrot. After we had walked about 54 miles the track ceased. We had been told that this would be the case, and as it turned out had very indifferent directions how to continue. Accordingly, we lost our way and wandered about the bush looking for the station till dark when there was nothing of it but to light a fire and make ourselves as comfortable as we could. We should have done very well, but we had nothing to eat or drink, as we finished all we had with us in the middle of the day. However, I slept very well, waking about every hour, rather cold, but I made up the fire and was soon asleep again. At daylight we began again to search for the station and hunted about for two hours to no purpose. We were getting very faint for the want of something to eat and drink so we thought the best plan would be to walk ten miles back to the next station, which we did. We were twenty-four hours without anything either to eat or drink. I was none the worse for it and am in perfect health. The climate and the exercise evidently agree with me.

BALLARAT, THURSDAY, MARCH 11, 1858

... We arrived here last night but I must go back to March 2nd (the day after our adventure in the bush) on which night we slept on the kitchen floor of the station we walked back to. The owner was not at home. The next morning, we started at daybreak with fresh directions for Mr Manifold's station, which we found without difficulty, as we had proper directions.

The house is very prettily situated on the bank of a freshwater lake, about two miles in length. The station belongs to two brothers, one of them is married, and they have a nephew and niece living with them. They have a splendid run with about 8000 head of cattle. They are very wealthy and have bought more than 50 000 acres of their run, and it is supposed that they will but is all, at not less than one pound an acre. They breed about 1500 head yearly and sell about 1200. They were very hospitable. We stayed with them till Monday March 8th. One day they drove us through part of their run in a dog cart with two horses. They went right through the bush, or what we would call in England a forest, without any road, dodging amongst the trees. We saw without exaggeration hundreds of kangaroos. They are very destructive on a run. They are very fond of rolling in the grass and leave an offensive smell, so that the cattle will not feed where they have been. The Manifolds are fencing in all their run.

We left the Manifolds on Monday the 8th. Their nephew drove us twenty-three miles on our way which was a great help as we only had seven to walk, and it was a burning hot day. We spent all that night in a small place called Cressy. Many of the places are composed merely of an inn and a few huts. The next day we walked to Rokewood, only 10 miles, plains all the way. It was a cool day, and we had some rain, the first since we started. The next day, which was yesterday, we came on here, 28 miles. I was in first-rate walking order. Forests all the way with beautiful heaths growing in them and birds of all descriptions. The first diggings we came to were about 14 miles from Ballarat in the middle of a forest, and they continued at intervals all the way. They are finding at present very little gold. Ballarat is a wonderful place. As you look at it from the hills around, you might fancy it is a large camp, tents, and huts in every direction.

I think we shall go overland to Sydney as we hear that we shall have no difficulty in doing so. I am very much pleased with what I have seen of this country, but I think that there will be more opening for me in the New South Wales district than in this. We have got along this far pretty cheaply and fared very well. The knife you gave me has been invaluable in every way. The saddles will come in very useful by and by. There have been a great many bushfires this summer. We have seen the smoke of several. Some squatters had the whole of their runs burnt, in which case they are obliged to sell all their stock.

Sydney, 20 May 1858

My dear Mother,

I left Albury April 9th and arrived in Sydney on the 27th. We walked the whole way. It is about 370 to 380 miles. We were sixteen days walking as we rested on Sundays.

... You will think that I ought to have more to say, having travelled so far since I last wrote, but one day was much like another although I was never tired of it. I had an object, and I could have walked for six months under the same circumstances. We generally started between six and eight in the morning. Sometimes we had to walk 15 or 20 miles before we came to an inn. In that case we lighted a fire after we had walked 10 or 12 miles, and made some tea, I was always carrying a tin pot for the purpose and tea and sugar, Cannon carrying a loaf of bread. In that way we did very well, but as we got nearer Sydney the inns became more frequent and we had no occasion for the tea. I have now walked nearly 800 miles and never once had a drop of rain on my coat. It is delightful having such fine weather day after day.

SYDNEY, 5 JUNE 1858

My dear Father,

Fortune favours me. The day after I last wrote to you, I called on George and William Macleay (cousins) to whom you will remember I had letters from Mrs Parson's friends. I told them my plans, etc., and the former wrote to his brother (who has a sheep station on the Murrumbidgee, about 400 miles from Sydney) to know if he could take me on his station to learn the business, etc. He received an answer yesterday to say he should be happy to do so, so I shall start on Tuesday next, the 8th. I have been in lodgings for the last three weeks. Cannon has gone on to Moreton Bay.

I lunch with Mr William Macleay tomorrow and start with the mail for his station. I go by rail as far as Campbelltown, 30 miles from Sydney, and then take the coach which leaves at 8 pm for Goulburn, 100 miles from Campbelltown. I can go by coach nearly all the way from the station ... Now you must know that the coaches here (if they deserve that name) are open. For about 200 miles it will be nothing but a kind of dog cart, carrying six persons, dreadful roads, reckless drivers, and a great part night driving. It may be accompanied by rain, not unlikely this time of the year. Four hundred miles of that kind of travelling in my opinion is rather too much of a good thing, and I think very likely

I shall walk part of the way. I should not have gone by the mail at all only Mr Macleay persuaded me to. People who can help it never think of walking here, the common saying is, 'If a man has to travel a mile, he will go two out of his way to catch his horse.'

Gundagai,
14 June 1858

My dear Father,

The coach was crammed. Two of Mr Macleay's friends were going the same way, so I had good company as far as Yass where they got out. I followed their example, having had enough for one dose, and determined by way of a rest to walk part of the way. I spent the greater part of the day in Yass and in the evening walked on to the next inn, eight miles.

We had various accidents in the coach, first, the two pole horses fell down, but were not hurt, and we were on again in twenty minutes. Then the pole broke twice, the traces once, etc., etc., etc.

20 July 1858

My dear Father,

You will be glad to hear that I find so much employment here, that this is the first good opportunity I have had of beginning a letter to you since I last wrote. I am at present by myself. Mr Macleay has gone to Wagga Wagga for a few days and Mr Clarke, Mr Morton and Overseer will all be out on different parts of the run till the end of the week. I am left here to administer to the wants of the shepherds, etc., nearest to the Head Station in the meantime; I shall have a ride of about 20 miles every day. I am in the saddle some part of almost every day, sometimes all day long. I enjoy it amazingly. The beginning of the second week I was here I went with Mr Clarke to the back of the run (about 25 miles) where they are forming a new station for some sheep, that were about to lamb. We remained out the whole week, living in a tent. We were very busy making bough yards for the sheep and riding over the country to discover the best place for them and for water which is very scarce in that country. We are on the south side of river. We were also out all last week, moving some of the sheep and making more bough yards. We carry our blankets with us. Three nights we slept in a kind of hut, which we formed from boughs, leaving one end open, where we lighted a large fire and slept as warmly and comfortably as possible. The life suits me to a T., and I never enjoy better health than when I am knocking about in the bush. There is plenty of good mutton and damper. Of the latter I am very fond. This is our winter, and the weather is delightful and a gallop in the morning under the bright blue sky and warm sun, and through the clear air is glorious. You don't know how I enjoy this perfect freedom.

CALLANDOON, MORETON BAY DISTRICT

3 FEBRUARY 1859

My dear Mother,

[describing journey to Callandoon] ... I made the Namoi at a Public House called 'Wee Waa' and continued on the same way, six miles up the river to a hut where I was to cross the river the next morning. There was only a blackfellow and his gin living at the hut who were employed cutting down the burrs. He was certainly a most respectable black. He gave me a first-rate supper, which consisted of fish he has just caught in the river, baked in the ashes. He was a most lively fellow, chatting away the whole time. He began, 'You know me not like other blackfellow, other blackfellow fool. Me half white fellow, live like white fellow. Any man come to my place me make him welkin.' He went on like that till after supper (we were outside the hut) when his gin suggested a game of cards, upon which he produced a very dirty pack and they began playing 'All-Fours' by the light of the fire, with great excitement. I laid down by the fire and was greatly amused watching their countenances. It was some time before they were tired of it but at last, they laid down by the fire and were soon asleep.

CALLANDOON, MORETON BAY DISTRICT

3 FEBRUARY 1859

My dear Father,

You will see by the heading of my letter that I am now in the

Moreton Bay district. Callandoon is a very extensive Sheep Station. I have been here about a month. They are now in the midst of shearing, and I have been invited to stay until it is over. You will, I am sure, approve of the step I have taken, in which there are unquestionable advantages to be gained. I have agreed to become a partner with Mr Macdonald the Superintendent of this Station. He is a young man about twenty-seven, a perfect gentleman in every respect, a man with whom I could agree admirably. He has the sole charge of this station with one hundred sheep and a few thousand head of cattle for two years. He is well acquainted with most of the stations in this district, and with the quantity of stock they produce, having constant dealing with them. He has been six years in the Colony and has during that time accumulated a small capital which he is anxious to invest in a sheep station. I am in that part of the country called the Darling Downs. It is considered the best in the Moreton Bay district and is certainly the best I have seen in the Colony, excepting only the Murrumbidgee and the Lachlan ... The only thing is they have not here as good a market, but that improves every year.

Chapter 4

THE DALRYMPLE EXPEDITION

Ernest Henry, Cloncurry, 1876

'You are in the right place at the right time and you're the right type of man to make the most of it. And, what's more, you'll enjoy it. This, I can assure, will be a great adventure – men and women will talk of it for centuries to come.'

That's how Dalrymple greeted me when we first met back in '59. I had just arrived in Brisbane, having brought a herd of horses up to the settlement from Sydney.

George Augustus Frederick Elphinstone Dalrymple. Dead now, so the newspapers say. Aged just forty-nine. I'm glad they mentioned the fact he had been elected a fellow of the Royal Geographical Society. He would have liked that. Mind you, there was so much he did during his life here that all Queenslanders owe him a real debt.

I'd known about Dalrymple's prospectus for his northern expedition even before I met him. I wanted to be part of his party to bring that project to fruition. He asked me what I'd done since I'd arrived in Australia three years ago.

I told him how, due to reasons of parsimony and curiosity about the Australian countryside, I had walked from Melbourne to Sydney. Then I further acquainted him with the fact that I had ridden, by myself, from Sydney to Brisbane to deliver horses to this northern township.

That seemed to assure Dalrymple of my horsemanship and bushcraft and was sufficient reason to make me suitable for his expedition of exploration in the Burdekin region. That, plus the fact that, like the other members of the syndicate, I was hungry to find and develop new lands for stocking with livestock.

'All we need from you now,' he advised me, 'is your £50 subscription to help cover the expenses of the expedition.'

I asked Dalrymple for more details on the syndicate.

'We calculate we will need a total of £1,000 to launch the expedition,' Dalrymple explained. 'We already have that well in hand and a number of the colony's leading men and companies are backing the venture.'

He went on to list them: Captain J. C. Wickham, R.N., Messrs J.C. White, John Douglas, Gilbert Davidson, P.N. Selheim, A.D. Broughton, George Perry, W. A. Simpson, A.H. Palmer, Garland and Bingham, J.B. Rundle, Joseph Sharp, D. McDougal, Raymond and Co., R. Towns and Co., Griffith, Fanning and Co., How, Walker and

Co., Dennison and Rolleston, F. Bundock, Edwd. Ogilvie, R. G. Watt and J. R. Radfort.

'It's land, Henry, and wealth in the promise for men of decision and determination,' said Dalrymple. 'If we succeed – and we surely shall – you will have your own kingdom that many in the Old Country could only dream of.'

Dalrymple looked at the maps he had placed on a large table in front of me.

'Right now,' he emphasised, 'there's more demand for beef than the market can meet. And, when it comes to sheep, there's just no room left in the settled areas for those who want to expand their holdings.'

'And then there's your moderate capitalists,' he continued. 'All the land down south has been taken up by the bigger land holders. There's a need to open more land and that's in the north. And Mitchell, Leichardt and Gregory's journals all tell us the Burdekin area is very promising.'

And, besides that, there was the possibility of minerals. Perhaps even gold.

'Come with us, lad, and you'll be first in the field. You will get first choice of what's available, the best pick of the land. Those who follow won't be as fortunate. You will have the front row seat.'

The expedition, he said, would explore those areas between the

22nd parallel of south latitude, the 137th degree of east longitude on the west and, on the north and east, by the ocean.

The party would be canvassing the whole frontier – all the way from the Valley of Lagoons down to the Barcoo River. It would cover the river systems within this vast area.

'We will be starting out from Leichardt's camp at Mt McConnell on the Burdekin. Then we will go by canoes down the river to get a better look at it, see its mouth, find out if there's a port there. Also, check out how far up the river can be navigated.'

'After that we will move to the lower Suttor, lower Cape and Burdekin Valley as far as the Valley of Lagoons. All the time we'll be looking out for good land where stations can be established. We'll come back by a different route to the settled areas, checking the Cape or Belyando River to its head. Then, when that's done, we intend dropping over the watershed into the Maranoa until we get back down to the settled areas.'

It seemed quite expensive at the time. But it was the best £50 I ever spent.

Chapter 5

EXPLORING THE BURDEKIN

GEORGE AUGUSTUS FREDERICK ELPHINSTONE DALRYMPLE

EXPLORER, PUBLIC SERVANT, PARLIAMENTARIAN, 1862

We made Henry the food fossicker on the Burdekin expedition which consisted in all, of eight men. And lucky we did, too, for he proved a most worthy forager of wild fowl and kangaroo.

That, of course, is not all Henry was good for. A first-class explorer he showed himself to be.

Plovers and ducks were among the birds Henry brought back to our campfires. On one occasion, as I recall, Henry managed the not inconsiderable feat of bagging four ducks and two coots with just one barrel. I told him I thought the birds of the Burdekin must be particularly suicidal.

The kangaroos he shot were always put to good use. We used to make stews and curries out of them and soup of the tails. It was excellent food.

Henry had a lot of help from his kangaroo dog, Spring. Spring would sometimes make the kill himself. Or he would bail the animal up until Henry, on his horse Nellie, would get close enough to take the shot. Those who know anything about kangaroos know at what speed they can bound through the bush and how evasive they can be when they have a mind to be so.

Henry had been following Spring on his horse when the dog ran the big kangaroo to a halt. But the animal was so big that Spring, prudently, had decided not to tackle him alone.

Henry dismounted and approached the kangaroo with his revolver. But the 'roo bolted, and Henry took a couple of shots at him. He hit the animal, but it took little notice of him. By this time the animal stood at bay among some rocks. Seeing his master approach, Spring took heart and flew at the 'roo. But Spring was rolled by the 'roo as Henry hurried towards his endangered dog. The 'roo then turned his attention to Henry.

The vicious animal was ready to take on Henry and, being some six feet tall, the animal would have given Henry quite a thrashing.

'Luckily, I had one bullet left in the revolver,' Henry told me. 'When he got to within a couple of yards of me, I shot him in the throat. That pulled him up.'

Henry has a most fond affection for his animals, and I saw him tending to Spring's wounds after that event. He also admired horses. His own was the best in the lot that we took north for the expedition. Nellie was of immense help to Henry as our group's huntsman. She was a beautiful half-bred Arab mare, a bay with a great deal of white about the face. Henry claimed, and I would not argue with him, that she was the pride of the mob when it came to both beauty and condition. She was also very plucky and ran like the wind.

Henry often talked about the 'nobility' of horses, how they would stretch and strain to work for their masters. He felt that for sure there must be a heaven where horses go when they die. I'm sure he hoped they did as there would be no greater pleasure for him to be 'in the saddle' in any afterlife.

It was as well we had the like of Henry on the job. We thought the expedition to the Burdekin would take some five months to complete. It took eight. By the end of it, we were running short on just about everything. Including food and ammunition.

Henry had been in Australia just two years when I met him. Still what you'd call a 'new chum'. And yet he had equipped himself so well in the bush. Which I regarded as quite an achievement as, prior to landing in the continent, he had been a sailor. I suspect, however, that he was more than familiar with horses before he took up that occupation.

Henry hated idleness. He was always on the go if he could do so. Always thinking ahead, wanting to grow his lot. He knew that the Burdekin offered him a chance to gain new land and move stock, which he had already lodged on the Dawson, to a new property and thus further develop his fortune.

He told me, once, that he regretted not having taken up smoking.

'It gives you a chance,' he said, 'to do something in those moments of enforced idleness.'

Henry's answer to those moments was to read. Wherever he went, he would carry with him whatever new books he could get. Or newspapers. And, more often than not, journals of the earlier explorers.

We had their journals; we had their maps. But there is a great deal of difference between what is drawn on paper and what you confront when you go out to follow those lines of ink on paper.

The eight months of our exploration took us as far north as Dr Leichardt's fabulous territory in the Valley of the Lagoons. We travelled the Burdekin, Suttor and Belyando valleys. We attempted, but could not, find the outlet of the Burdekin to see if it offered a port potential and if it were navigable. When you look at a map, all the territory seems well laid out and 'flat', rather like directions along streets in a town or city. Exploring is nothing like that at all, largely because so much is unknown. And it's not a process of going from point A to point B.

Exploring usually involves great distances and substantial time. So you have to prepare assiduously for that, to consider and plan for contingencies. Some you can anticipate. Others arise out of nowhere, when you are hundreds, maybe thousands of miles away from the nearest point of civilisation. It is therefore a great advantage to have party members who can plan ahead and surmount those obstacles that cannot be foreseen. We were lucky to have such men on the expedition to the Burdekin. Not the least of them was Henry.

He was steadfast in tackling all the expedition pitted against us.

In the unknown terrain, you can find yourself 'bushed' – your path cut off by impenetrable scrub, ravines, rivers in flood or, as trying as anything, thirst without knowing if you are going to find water on the path you're travelling. Horses get lost and you have to go searching for them amongst the bush and the hills. Food, as I have stated, is another thing, and Henry's ability and determination helped to provide that necessity as well as the meeting many other challenges we faced. You need to persevere, to track and backtrack and try new routes where the first or the second or third prove impassable.

Henry would not let anything overpower or overwhelm him.

But even in adversity, there is some levity. It happened while we were on the Suttor. Henry had bedded down at night near the campfire to keep himself warm.

Unfortunately, he picked the downside of the fire to lay his bed. In the middle of the night, we were all awoken to see Henry doing a wild dance in the almost dark. It looked so comic we could not help laughing as he dashed around trying to put out a fire in his coat. It appears that a log from the fire had rolled down onto his bedding and set that, and Henry, alight. When the fire was completely out, Henry was unhurt but sported a huge burn in his jacket. Eventually, even he saw the funny side of the incident.

Another trying aspect of our journey was the activities of the aborigines in these areas. They seem, generally, to be a bigger race of people than those in the southern areas of Queensland. They are also more hostile.

On many occasions we had little trouble with the blacks. They seemed to be terrified when they first came upon white men. They would flee, sometimes leaving all their goods behind them. But the blacks did make repeated attacks on our small party. It is no small thing to say that, despite this, by the end of our expedition, we – our six white men and two blackboys – all returned safely. But there were anxious occasions.

One of those was towards the end of the expedition. And it was occasioned, in the first instance, not by the blacks but by other white men. One of the things you have to be prepared for, in such pioneering, is that others may try to capitalise on your efforts. We had become aware that another party of white men were following up along our ground-breaking path and that they, seeing what we had already found, might try to claim the pastures we wanted as our own.

To forestall this, it was decided that Henry and another member of the party, Hood, together with the two blackboys, should hasten to Rockhampton with tenders for the country we had marked out.

Henry and the others set out for Rockhampton on 1 November 1859. They took three pack horses with them, two carrying provisions for one month, the third carrying blankets and other items. They had a spare horse and took Henry's dog, Spring, with them.

Two days after setting out they came upon a small number of blacks, but these quickly disappeared as the party approached. A little further on they came upon a blackfellow and his gin, both fishing in a waterhole. Both dived into the water and disappeared among some reeds in the water. The party, not wishing to frighten the blacks, moved on.

Farther on the party encountered a whole mob of aborigines. Approximately a dozen gins jumped into a waterhole with their babies on their backs. The gins kept diving down and coming up almost immediately, frightened they might drown their children.

Again, the party retreated.

The party had got about half a mile from the camp when they heard loud cooees in their wake. They were being followed by a number of men beating their spears and other weapons. The blacks then began running not just behind them but also alongside them.

The party found, because the land was so scrubby, that they were unable to disperse the aborigines. As soon as Henry and his men stopped, the aborigines dived behind trees.

The party continued with the intent of dispersing the mob as soon as some good open country presented itself.

After another 10 miles, the party decided to camp for lunch. They chose an open spot beside a small lagoon. There were also three very large trees growing together and this would provide them with some protection, should they need it. With the arms that the party held, however, they were confident they could repel any attack by the natives. Their main worry was that the blacks would track them until night.

As Henry's party moved on, a thunderstorm erupted in the afternoon and that seemed to dampen the spirit of the pursuers. In fact, the party heard nothing of the blacks until November 8th, their fifth day on the track back to Rockhampton.

'They came yelling out of the scrub on our left,' Henry later told me. 'Between it and the river on our right, was a narrow strip of open land. The blacks were coming up that strip. That gave us the clear field of action we required. Hood and I turned our horses' heads and galloped, on which they took to their heels and fled into the scrub, and we saw no more of them. It was the closest thing I have ever experienced to being in a cavalry charge.'

There is an interesting footnote to our exploration of the Burdekin. As I said, Henry was to go ahead of our party to lodge the necessary papers for tendering for the country we had explored. We were determined that, having put all the hard work into this, the party that was now following in our footsteps would not capitalise on our endeavours.

So, Henry hastened to Rockhampton and then on to Sydney. We had started out our expedition when the Burdekin was part of New South Wales. By the time we had finished our job, the Crown Colony of Queensland, of which the Burdekin was a part, had been separated from New South Wales. But Sydney still seemed to be the place to lodge our claims, so Henry sped overland to Rockhampton and thence by ship to Sydney to ensure our prime claims.

Unfortunately for him, and for us, the new Queensland

governor-designate, Sir George Bowen, had left Sydney five days prior to Henry's arrival in Sydney. Sir George was coming north to Queensland, bearing the charter of Queensland's independence.

It was the fact that we were now in a new colony that would cause us many anxious moments regarding our land claims.

Chapter 6

REASSURANCE

———◆◆◆———

Ernest Henry,

Brisbane, February 1860

We were in danger of losing our land before we even got it. After eight months of danger and hardship and risk, it now seemed that the land we had explored and mapped and claimed for our own would be denied to us.

And all because, when we started the expedition, the Burdekin was part of New South Wales and, when we got back, it was part of Queensland. So, the claims we put in for runs in the Burdekin region were now being treated with suspicion, if not ill-disguised hostility.

The syndicate that backed the expedition was Sydney-based. This made little difference while we were all part of New South Wales. But we had now separated and had become an entirely different colony.

And local attitudes had markedly changed within twelve months. There was now a cry being heard that 'southern speculators' should not profit from Queensland pastures.

To say the least, I was concerned. I was alarmed. I was, in fact, more than a little angry that the authorities of the new colony were unmindful that people such as Dalrymple and myself were the ones who had made the investment and taken the risks to open this new territory.

And we had plans for that land which in no way could be regarded as speculative. It was our intent to stock and develop the land that we had, with no little hardship, uncovered.

And now we were faced with a new colony, a new executive, a new legislature and an emerging view on land usage and tenure which may not allow us to achieve the goals for which we had worked so hard.

These were the things uppermost in my mind was I went to meet our new – the colony's first – Governor, Sir George Bowen. I was most pleased to have an interview with Sir George and was determined to raise my concerns with him.

Sir George, everybody said, was an extremely interesting man. He has, of course, been the main topic of conversation among the people of Brisbane, and beyond, since he arrived here last year. Since then, his name has been on everyone's lips. He's over thirty but not yet forty and, given that, he still has a great zest for life. A robust man, you'd call him. Solid of build, eyes that engage you as if he's interested in everything you have to say. Yet a man of his own definite ideas.

A lot of the colonists have already got to know him. He makes it his business to get to meet as many people as he can in this new Colony he's come to govern. And, not surprisingly, he seems very popular across the broad population.

When we met, he told me how impressed he had been by the civic welcome he received when he first arrived. Usually, such events are staged by the local military, turning out in full regalia. But this welcome had been organised, and funded, by the local dignitaries and, it was evident, he said, that there was great loyalty to and support for the Queen. Some 4 000 people, including 2 000 from the country outside Brisbane, welcomed Sir George to the new colony.

The Governor's arrival here was obviously a remarkable occasion. A most popular event and, even now, the Brisbane booksellers are doing a brisk trade in re-prints of the booklet highlighting his arrival and civic reception. I noticed a copy of it in Pugh's Bookselling shop. It is selling at sixpence a copy.

'It was the Queen, herself, who selected the name Queensland for the new colony,' Sir George told me.

Getting to know Sir George became the main pastime of many in the colony. We quickly knew that he had been recommended for the position by Lord Bulwyer Lytton, the then Secretary of State for the Colonies. We were all also aware that the Queen had made him a KCMG ... And that he had married into Venetian nobility.

His wife, Countess Diamantina Roma, is the daughter of His Highness Count Candiano Roma, GCMG, President of the Ionian Senate, a nobleman of the ancient Venetian family, possessed of large estates in the island of Zante. From all reports she is, through her charming involvement with the people, already a favourite both in Brisbane and even further abroad. Her passion is gardening, and I'm told she has great plans for the new Government House to be built at the end of George Street, across from the Botanical Gardens.

Dalrymple had already seen and reported to the Governor on our expedition to explore the Burdekin River and its estuaries. In fact,

Bowen had interviewed him almost as soon as Dalrymple returned to Brisbane.

And Dalrymple advised me that the Governor was interested, also, in speaking to other members of the expedition. I was happy to speak with Sir George.

'What's he like?' I had asked Dalrymple prior to going to the Governor's official residence.

'I must admit he proved a very interesting man to talk to,' said Dalrymple. 'He is very much in favour of exploration and opening the country. He loves the detail of what we did and saw while we were in the north.'

He was, Dalrymple advised me, someone who had an appreciation of what we had experienced. That, to some extent, eased my concerns about our new land submissions.

'He won't claim that it's anywhere near the difficulties that we went through, but he's a man who, himself, has set out to explore the world.'

This caught my interest as, although I had heard much of this man of letters, of his intellectual achievements, his honours in classical studies and his acclaimed stewardship of his time in the Ionian Isles, I did not know of him being a man of action in the wilderness.

'Wilderness is probably not the right word to describe where Sir George has been but it's not too far adrift,' Dalrymple said.

'During his time in Greece, for instance,' Dalrymple continued, 'he made an extensive tour on horseback throughout Greece and that resulted in his publishing the *Handbook on Greece*. It's a travellers' guide to the whole region.'

Bowen, he added, was also the author of *Mount Athos, Thessaly and Epirus*.

'He wrote that after a journey from Constantinople to Corfu, right across the provinces of European Turkey,' Dalrymple stated. 'He, like us, is an explorer and it's easy to see that he is particularly interested in the work we've been doing.'

What Dalrymple had told me about Bowen was most exact and I found Sir George very interested in every detail of the Burdekin expedition. A lot, of course, he had already learned from Dalrymple in their earlier conversations.

After an extensive discourse, Sir George expressed his gratitude for the work undertaken by our expedition.

'You,' he said, 'like all those on the expedition, are one of the pioneers of civilisation. Not too many people outside of Australia realise the task we face here in Queensland. You may already know the dimensions of this vast colony. Close to 670 000 square miles of territory. Most of it is untravelled and certainly unmapped. Before we can achieve our potential – and I have every faith that Queensland will be a major part of the Empire – we have to explore it to populate it.'

I was very pleased to hear Sir George's appreciation of our efforts and, based on what he said, I broached a subject near to my heart.

'Sir,' I said, 'our expedition has, as you say, walked the wilderness and found great lands that can significantly contribute to the future of Queensland. But, as you may also be aware, the submissions we have forwarded for land there – land that we wish to take up and stock – has been frustrated by the change of political circumstances this colony has seen in the past year.'

The Governor sat back in his seat, saying nothing, and I took this as an invitation to proceed further.

'When we set out on the expedition, our syndicate had the expectation from the New South Wales government that, having undertaken the exploration we would have first choice of land in the areas we had explored. But, with the separation of Queensland from New South Wales, we now find that may not be the case. We all, of course, welcome the separation for that by its very self will promote the growth of the north. But the present situation, I'm sure you will appreciate, leaves those of us in the expedition in great uncertainty.'

'I readily appreciate your situation,' Sir George replied. 'And, given what service you have provided, it would be a great pleasure for me to advise you that you will, in fact, be granted the rights to stock the land you've selected.'

'However,' he continued, 'I do not have the power, and do not seek it, to be the arbitrator of such matters.'

He said this not in an admonishing way but rather as someone trying to explain a particular set of circumstances to me.

'Queensland has been established as a self-governing colony, a democratic entity,' he said. 'The matter of land and its tenure is uppermost in the colony's mind. But, I reiterate, we are a democracy – in fact, Queensland is the first British colony to start out with such status. Created as a democracy, with the decisions that frame its future in the hands of its own people.'

He looked out, for a moment, over the city's botanic gardens where, on his arrival at Brisbane, he had been warmly welcomed by the populace.

'You know,' he said, 'when I arrived here our colony had just 8 ½ d in the Treasury. Not much in the pockets, is it? But what we do have in abundance is land.'

The Queensland government, he said, would be remiss if it did not take great care in establishing how that land could be put to the best use for both the individuals seeking land and for the colony as a whole.

'But,' he added, 'I don't want you to be glum about what I am saying.

You are the very type of person that our future will depend on, and I am most confident that you will continue to play a major part in that future and that you will prosper along with Queensland.'

Chapter 7

THE GOVERNOR'S REPORT

GOVERNOR GEORGE BOWEN,
FIRST GOVERNOR OF QUEENSLAND.
LETTER TO THE DUKE OF NEWCASTLE,
THE SECRETARY OF STATE FOR THE COLONIES
GOVERNMENT HOUSE, BRISBANE, QUEENSLAND,
12 APRIL 1860

My Lord Duke,

With reference to my despatch No. 21, of February 16th, ultimo, I have the honour to report that Mr George Elphinstone Dalrymple has returned in safety from the exploring expedition which he had undertaken to the north-eastern districts of this colony.

Mr Dalrymple states that he has considerably extended the

knowledge already obtained by the research of Leichardt, Gregory, and Kennedy, of the rich and well-watered pastoral districts near the rivers Burdekin, Suttor and Belyando, between the parallels 19° and 22° of south latitude.

He further informs me that he has discovered that the great river Burdekin flows into the Pacific Ocean, at a point a short distance north of Cleveland Bay, and not near Cape Upstart, as was conjectured by the late Dr Leichardt.

Should it be found that the mouth of the Burdekin is accessible to steam navigation, a great facility will be afforded for the rapid occupation of the neighbouring interior. To ascertain this point, it will be necessary that an expedition properly equipped should be sent by sea, at the expense of Government. Mr Dalrymple offers to take charge of a fresh exploring party, and I feel persuaded that the Queensland Parliament will be disposed, on my recommendation, to vote a sum of money in support of this important enterprise. I have communicated with Governor-General Sir William Denison as to the aid which might be given by Her Majesty's surveying ship Herald, now on the Australian station, but am informed that that vessel has been ordered home.

As the pastoral settlements of Queensland already extend within the Tropical circle, as far as the shores of Broad Sound, in about the 22nd degree of South latitude, there is little doubt that the new territory, of which Mr Dalrymple speaks so favourably, will be stocked with sheep and cattle in the course of a very few years. Much of it is tableland, enjoying a cool and salubrious climate.

The aborigines in that part of the colony are reported as being very numerous and hostile, and as exhibiting more athletic frames and somewhat higher order of intellect than the native tribes in these parts of Australia, where the climate is less genial, and where fish, game, and edible plants of various kinds are less abundant. Still, the six Englishmen who composed Mr Dalrymple's party, though often attacked, were able to force their way through all opposition without the loss of a single individual of their number. Consequently, there is every reason to expect that a few detachments of the mounted police-force, in aid of the energetic measures of self-defence adopted by the colonists themselves, will, in that quarter as elsewhere, suffice for the protection of any new settlement.

It has been rightly observed that from the circumstance of the aborigines of this island-continent being, apparently, subject to no sort of government except that of the strongest man in each tribe, from the imperfection of their arms, and from their mental incapacity for combination, their collisions with Europeans do not occupy that place in the annals of Australia which is filled by the Maoris in the annals of New Zealand, and by the semi-civilised Mexicans and Peruvians, or even by the Red Indians, in the history of America.

I hope and believe that there is another and better cause for the comparative infrequency of serious collisions with the aborigines in Queensland and in the other Australian colonies. I allude to the humane and enlightened treatment which they now receive at the hands of the English Colonial authorities and of the settlers, who, while they energetically repel attacks on their own lives and property, seem always ready to employ, feed and clothe the peaceful members of the neighbouring tribes. In fact, on almost all the pastoral stations in Queensland, several blacks are maintained as shepherds, stockmen, and grooms;

others are enrolled by Government in the Native Mounted Police; while in the towns, as many as are willing to work can earn their livelihood as porters, messengers, woodcutters, and in other similar capacities. Efforts have also been made at the public expense, at various times and places, for the education of the aborigines, and for their conversion to Christianity; and I expect that these endeavours will be energetically resumed by the Government of Queensland, with the sanction of the Colonial Legislature.

Chapter 8

HUGHENDEN

*Ernest Henry's reminiscences on his discovery of 'Hughenden',
northwest Queensland in November 1863. Henry, who already
held a number of properties including Mt. McConnell on the
Burdekin River, was seeking further good grazing country to
further develop his rural holdings.*

A year or two previous, several parties had been despatched from
different parts of Australia, in search of the long-lost Leichardt
and his party, whose fate, even to this day, has not be ascertained. It
was in consequence of the glowing reports made by members of two
of these search parties that determined us to steer for the head of the
Flinders River, which empties itself into the Gulf of Carpentaria.

We (myself and Mr Devlin) made our start from Mt McConnell
Station, taking with us but one blackboy. We call them all boys,
regardless of age; ours was, probably, some twenty-three or twenty-
four years old.

For the first 80 or 90 miles we had the advantage of a track, which led us to Natal Downs, the farthest out station, and the only one on our route, being situated on the Cape River.

From thence our course was determined by compass and the nature of the country. I can remember nothing of interest to narrate in connection with our outward journey.

We had to camp one night without water in what is now known as the desert, being a belt of sandy country some 30 or 40 miles wide, slightly timbered, but waterless. It is covered in Triodia or Spinifex, which grows in tussocks and is very inflammable, even when green. The shoots are round and their points, when matured, almost as sharp as needles. The pastern joints of horses become very sore after travelling through a long stretch of such country. Spinifex is peculiar to the western and northern districts, and, when not too plentiful, is an acquisition on a run-in time of drought, for if burnt down will spring again, rain or no rain, and when young, stock are very fond of it.

After a journey of some 200 miles through much indifferent and worthless country, the valley of the Flinders broke suddenly on our view and raised our expectations to a high degree, for, though at this point the valley is confined amongst somewhat broken country, we could see stretches of open downs in the distance, which experience told us was first class pasturage.

We now descended from the tableland into the valley, crossed the river, ran it down for a few miles, and camped for the night on its dry sandy bed, considerably elated with the probable prospect before us.

Early the next morning, Devlin and I left the blackboy in charge of our camp, with instructions to keep a good lookout for the natives, and gave him a pistol, double-barrelled gun, and a carbine for defence.

We then recrossed the river, passed up a narrow defile, which formed a gap in a low range close to and trending along the bank of the river.

On reaching the summit of this gap, no scene could be more gratifying to the eye of a pastoralist than that which burst upon our sight.

Below us was a lovely valley of undulating downs, studded here and there with groups and belts of graceful myall trees, whose shadows were thrown far over the green herbage by the rising sun. The grass had evidently been burnt off a few weeks previously, but now clothed the rising and falling ground with the very richest pasture, trackless and undisturbed by a single hoof.

A small creek, whose winding course is indicated by the trees that grow on either bank, trends northward through the centre of the valley, which latter, to the south, narrows picturesquely amongst the hills; on the west, it is bounded by another low range, only a few miles distant; while, to the north, it widens out and joins the extensive valley of the river, along whose course open downs stretch far away, unbroken, save by narrow belts of timber.

A railway has since been built through this country and the iron horse shrieks down that once-sequestered little valley; settlement, too, has marred its beauty and its pasture is continually fed and trodden down.

Never again will it wear its virgin loveliness. Ages hence, when the world becomes more densely populated and men shall prize what is beautiful more than what is profitable, it may be adorned by art; gardens and crops may replace its natural herbage, irrigated from artesian wells, but no eye will ever again behold it in its wild, silent, solitary beauty, as we saw it that early morning, bathed in the light of the rising sun.

Chapter 9

Chapter 9

THE RACE

Never underestimate Ernest Henry.

That's what I learned the first time we ever met.

Out on the plains it was. Heading for new land to stake out properties.

I thought him a remarkable man. Nothing else he did, his ups or his downs, ever made me change my mind on that. It was my good fortune to have him as both a friend and business partner.

Our first meeting was a fleeting one back in the early 1860s – around Christmas 1863 if my memory serves me right.

That was back in the days of the big land claims when the wave of settlement was pushing north, to the Gulf of Carpentaria. The race was on to grab the great northern grazing lands that were then unsettled and, to tell the truth, virtually unexplored.

If you wanted such lands, you had to go out and find them first.

And it was a race. Down in the south the move was to closer settlement. The big runs in those places were being broken down to make land available to the smaller property holders.

So those who had the big runs were looking for new pastures. And what was available was up north.

Our new Premier, in fact our first Premier, Robert Herbert, was quick to capitalise on this ... to set up the legislation that would help develop and populate Queensland.

We'd just become separated from New South Wales, and it was no secret that there was damned all in the State's coffers. But, if we didn't have much ready capital, there was one thing we had plenty of and that was land.

Herbert's government was determined to overcome the abuse of the New South Wales legislation which had given rise to 'map-graziers' ... Speculators who took up leases on large parcels of land without any intention of developing their runs.

In Queensland, if you wanted to make a claim on land you had to occupy it. You had to have your stock on the ground to make the claim. Within nine months, the law said, you had to stock the land to a quarter of its carrying capacity. Then, and only then, could you make application for a fourteen-year lease.

Which was what I was doing. Making my way towards the Gulf country which, according to William Landsborough's account, held much promise. Landsborough was one of our noted early explorers. He had been through the Gulf territory in 1862 on one of the several fruitless searches for any survivors of the Burke and Wills expedition.

It was Landsborough's glowing reports of the country he had traversed that led men such as me to make long journeys in search of new pastures.

I was coming up through the Burdekin territory with my stock when I see these two horsemen – one a young man and an older gentleman – riding towards us. Just the two on horses. No stock or anything else.

I knew straight away we were in luck, that what we had heard was true, that the land to the north and west – where we wanted to go – was being explored. And now our move would be made all the easier. All we had to do, now, was to follow the tracks that these two men, if they were who we thought they were, had laid down.

Follow their footprints – or, more accurately, their hoof prints – to the new pastures. We were in the vanguard. We would win the prize, the pick of the new country.

I thought no more about these two men. We had enough on our hands at the time. The wet was starting to set in and digging the dray out of bogs and getting cattle across flooded streams somewhat preoccupied us.

For someone who hasn't experienced it, it's hard to imagine such difficulties. Drays are carrying loads – a ton or more of equipment. They're being pulled by a dozen bullocks along, at best, unmade roads. The wheels are ploughing a foot or two deep into the mud. And, at a creek, it's nothing for the dray to sink to its axel into the mud.

It was eight days later, just on dusk and on Torrens Creek, when we noticed the same young fellow we had seen earlier. I was to learn that this was Ernest Henry, and he led a group moving some 800 head of cattle towards the same region we were heading for.

He passed us at a distance. He waved and we waved back. In fact, we cheered, for it was no mean feat that he had been able to mobilise his own team and outpace us in such a short time.

Part of the reason he was able to catch us, I have no doubt, was the poor condition of our cattle. We had been on the track a considerable time – all the way from northern New South Wales – before we reached Mt McConnell and our herd was tired. Nevertheless, I still expected to outstrip Henry. I just didn't bank on his determination.

Later, when I got to know Henry, when we'd both settled in the Flinders area, he told me he'd been up trying to find new territory when we crossed paths the first time. When he saw our party, he realised he needed to move fast. We had actually met him on his property – Mt McConnell on the Burdekin River. He rapidly mustered his cattle, loaded up a horse and a bullock dray and moved out to overtake me.

Like me, he wanted to be first – to choose the best land.

Years later we laughed about all the things that could go wrong on such a drive.

'It would have been easier if my brother, Arthur, was at Mt McConnell,' Henry told me. 'But he was on a neighbouring station so I sent a message to him, telling him what I was doing and asking him to bring more stock as soon as he could.'

Just four miles out on his journey, the bullock dray, which Henry himself was driving, got bogged in a creek.

'We had to take all the loading off and carry it over the creek,' Henry said. 'That delayed us somewhat.'

The weather was so bad, the light so pitiful that Henry's party found it difficult to know where they were at times. At the Suttor River the water was so high they decided to unload the dray, carry the stores across and then bring the empty dray through the water.

During most days, and nights, it rained. Fearful thunderstorms made it hard to keep the cattle together. You would camp on land that was clear and, less than half an hour later it would be under water. And try building a fire! It was a waste of time.

Henry and I, in fact, got together in that non-stop downpour. We spent a day or so riding up and down flooded creeks trying to find ways to get across them.

Hughenden – that's what he called his new station when he got it going – was to be his fourth station in the north. He'd already established properties on the Dawson, at Conway and the Burdekin. It was his idea to get in first, build up these properties, then sell them off to the next wave coming north.

He was ambitious. And optimistic. And it was always backed by his hard work and determination.

But when things turned bad, he lost the lot. Some never forgave him for his failure. I don't think Henry ever forgave himself for not succeeding.

Chapter 10

STARTING AGAIN

Roger Sheaffe, 1890

We plan and strain for success. We are measured by how much we achieve. And yet success so often depends on a hairsbreadth sliver of fate. Too much rain or too little. How did the market repay our endeavours? Or did the mail come through in time for us to make that critical decision on which our future hinged?

Success depends as much on times, tides, and temperatures as anything. I know for I, too, have felt that sliver.

No, I think a much better measure of a person's worth is how he handles failure.

The crash left Henry with little more than the clothes he wore. It wasn't just Henry. A lot of those who had pioneered the new territory were broken men. Ruined, they left the lands they'd fought so hard for.

Their dreams died with the financial crash of 1866 when a number of English banks failed. There was, in fact, a glut of wool on the English market. Wool had no value whatsoever.

At the end of it all, Henry was pinning his hopes on winning a lawsuit concerning one of his four properties – that at Conway. He won that suit but to no avail. The other party was engulfed by the same set of circumstances. They, too, were broke.

So, in all, Henry lost all: his land on the Dawson, that in Hughenden, the area he pioneered and, what he regarded as the keystone to his pastoral kingdom – Mt McConnell on the Burdekin River. How he loved that property. What great plans he had had for it – not just the property itself but how he could use it to grow into other runs and build up a pastoral empire.

I've seen it too often when things go bad. People always have somebody or something to blame for their failure. And, too often, they fold in on themselves and, it seems, shrivel from what they had been.

But not Henry. Failure spurred him on to greater efforts.

They looked a ragged pair when they turned up at my property, Minnamere on the Flinders in April of 1866 – Henry and his blackboy, Dick. Dick had been with Henry since the time Henry had established the Dawson run. Dick, about eighteen years old by this time, had been with Henry for all that time and I know, for a fact, that Henry had the utmost faith in the Aboriginal lad. I wondered, later on, how Dick felt about what had happened to Henry.

'So, what do you want to do now?' I asked Henry after we'd gone inside the hut and had a cup of tea.

'What do I *want* to do?' said Henry, his hands still around the metal mug. 'Most of all I'd like to go home.'

'Home?' I said, not understanding where, precisely, Henry meant.

For he had lost everything he had worked so hard to establish.

'To England, to Sussex, to Blackdown,' Henry replied. 'Most of all, I want to see my father and mother – it seems so long ago that I left.'

It was a long time. At just twenty, Henry had emigrated to Australia. That was almost ten years ago, ten years of unrelenting energy and exertion, of adventures based on a vigour few men display. Henry was heartily homesick.

'So, this is what you *will* do?'

'I want to, I wish to, but I *won't*. I cannot – I can't go home empty handed.'

Part of Henry's burden, I knew, was the family money he had used to finance his ventures. Then there were his brothers, Arthur and Alfred who had come from England to join him on his runs. His first obligation had been to pay back the borrowed money and to help his brothers into other jobs.

'What will you do then?' I asked.

'What else can you do? You start all over again. But this time I will do it differently.'

Henry got up from the table and looked out on the day. The seasons were changing and no longer were the days' heat hazy. Soon the cold of this unprotected, limitless plain country would sweep across the land. But today it was neither an extreme of heat nor cold.

He turned back and walked towards me, stopping just short of the table at which I sat.

'Look,' he said, 'I don't want you feeling sorry for me because of what has happened.'

'I failed,' he continued, 'and I failed for any number of reasons. What's happened has been hard to accept but it's taught me things too. I've done things that were rash. My ambition was too eager – not one, not two but four properties within a decade of knowing nothing about this country and little about the industry.'

'And I'm sure you'll do just that,' I said, and I could not help a grin that had busted out on my face. 'So, tell me what you're going to do and what, if anything, I can do to help you.'

We spoke on through the rest of the day and into the night until it was more like conspiring than conversing.

If I was interested, he said, he planned heading into the northwest area of Queensland to see if there were fresh pastures for new runs. He would find new land if I was prepared to stock it.

Some might have thought me a risk-taker because I said 'Yes'. But I knew Henry – in both success and failure. And, besides, I liked the man. I trusted him.

It was the start of a business partnership that would take in more than land and sheep and cattle and minerals.

He and Dick left the next day. It was a severely chill day – an early and abrupt start to winter. The winds snapped at both man and beast and the two men left, each wrapped in blankets.

Once again Ernest Henry was going on before me. My thoughts clicked back to that day on the Hughenden plains where Henry and his herd had beaten us to the promised pastures. On that day our party could not help but raise a loud cheer for him as he passed by.

As Henry and his native companion moved off to the west, I was tempted, once again, to cheer him on in his quest.

Chapter 11

A DANGEROUS PLACE

WILLIAM LANDSBOROUGH, EXPLORER, PUBLIC SERVANT

1884

Henry was in a predicament and I, I'm afraid, had put him there. Surrounded by savages he was. Encircled on the beach. And, armed with spears and rocks they were closing in on him.

He drew his revolver which, thankfully, he had taken with him on that walk.

And then he remembered my words to him, and the rest of the party of exploration: 'Don't shoot the natives, we're trying to make friends with them.'

This was back in the mid 60s – about 1866 I think – when Henry was very active in mineral exploration.

He had ridden from the Cloncurry area to Burketown which was the only Gulf port operating at that time and where I was the local administrator.

Henry arrived at Burketown just as the town had erupted into a fever epidemic. The township, in fact, had only been up and running for a year or so at that time.

The town was raw. It was, in fact, a magnet for anyone who had reason to escape the eyes of the law. There were some decent people among the port that had been set up to help get the Gulf properties supplied. Old O'Connor, for instance, turned up there in the same year, sixty-six. Formerly a police officer, he'd retired from the force to start up a store in the new place. He later went on to be the Burketown postmaster. But he took one look at the local inhabitants and recognised many of them as known to him in his previous profession. He knew, too, that there were a lot of outstanding warrants attached to various persons in the area.

There was, in fact, a great deal of lawlessness because of this element. Drunkenness, gambling, and fighting were commonplace. These scoundrels wanted nothing to do with civilising influences. Which accounted for their brazen destruction of property, notably the destruction of local water closets.

Although being the local police magistrate, I could do little to stop them the day they decided to burn down the Crown Lands Office water closet.

A lot of that lawlessness came to an end when Lieutenant D'arcy Uhr of the Queensland Mounted Police was stationed in Burketown. A determined man, Uhr was the officer who chased down and arrested some local horse stealers. To catch them, he had to pursue them all the way to the New South Wales border.

But he was also ruthless with the blackfellows in our area, and many give him credit for the dispersal of several mobs in the region. He eventually retired from the Mounted Police after being demoted. He was under a bit of a cloud.

But, for the moment, Uhr was on hand to help out with the devastating event that struck Burketown in 1866.

It was our severe misfortune, that year, to have a visit from a vessel that had, immediately prior to its arrival in Burketown, stopped in a plague port in Java.

We knew we were in for a rough time. All the vessel's crew died of the plague. And then it attacked the people of Burketown. In all, some sixty townspeople died over the next week. We thought it was some type of yellow fever. Whatever it was, it was swift and deadly.

In the midst of all this, Henry rode into town. He had been warned about the fever as he was entering the town and told to flee from the disease. Nevertheless, he decided to ride into the town to see how he could help.

I told him if he knew anything about boats, he could help me in my planned evacuation of the survivors to Sweers Island about 80 miles into the Gulf of Carpentaria. Sweers had already been used as a place for holding some of the apprehended criminals who inhabited the area. Henry informed me of his naval background, and I readily enlisted his assistance.

Once on the island, we made camp for the evacuees and then, as a precaution, we sent out a scouting party to ensure if there were any native inhabitants on the island and ascertain if they were hostile.

Henry was among those who did locate native inhabitants and tried to make friends with them. But they were evasive.

Later the same day, when we were back in camp, Henry left the rest of our party to walk down to the beach. When he got there, he found a group of three blacks at the water's edge. They immediately picked up rocks and made menacingly towards Henry. Henry, in the face of this, made friendly gestures. That didn't work. So, then he broke out into laughter. The natives stopped, puzzled for a moment, and then lowered the rocks they were holding.

Henry, so he told me later, thought he was doing quite well in this new business of making friends. Then he realised that the three blacks in front of him had been joined by another group that had come up behind him.

He looked around for help but none of the rest of us was in sight.

That's when he drew his revolver and was just ready to use it when he recalled my prohibition of firearms use.

In desperation Henry raised his revolver, he pointed it straight at the native he thought was the group's leader and ran up the beach towards that man, shouting as he did so.

The native, caught off guard, backed away quickly and the circle was broken. Henry continued up the beach until he emerged through the black's ranks and we, grabbing our own arms, rushed down to the beach to investigate.

The blacks, seeing our advent, quickly decamped along the beach.

After seeing what had occurred, I redefined my direction to Henry and others advising them they should not use their firearms *unless their own lives were endangered.*

It was, indeed, a very smart, calm, and courageous act by Henry that saved imminent bloodshed – both his own and probably also those of the local natives.

But Henry was to face yet more hardship and life-threatening danger as part of the Sweers Island expedition. He now became a fever victim himself. He was in the fever's grip for ten whole days. The acute neuralgia he suffered left him screaming in agony.

It was the ministrations of his faithful blackboy, Dick, who had been with him for so many years that helped Henry recover.

Dick laid Henry down on some grass and erected a bark cover to keep Henry out of the sun. We had no medicines whatsoever save for a supply of Perry Davis' Painkillers. Dick rubbed this into Henry at various times throughout the day and night. Henry tossed in delirium and agony and, whenever these episodes reached a peak, Dick would use more of the medicine on Henry.

Eventually the fever subsided, and Henry decided to get away from the coastal fever area and back to the drier inland territory, to his cousin, Robert Grey, at Hughenden. It was a 500-mile ride but, with Dick at his side, he moved off.

He told me later that, on the first day out, he fell off his horse twice.

'On the second day, however, I fell only once,' he added.

Chapter 12

DICK'S STORY

DICK, ERNEST HENRY'S ABORIGINAL 'BOY', 1867

We'd been together for a long time, me and Henry. Covered a lot of territory since we first teamed up. Down the Dawson way that was.

Can't say what got us together, really. Perhaps the way I handled horses. Loved them, I did. Just loved being in the saddle. And he did too. I could see that, right off.

'Cause, I was a lot younger then. Plenty of energy. Strong too. Ready to have a go at just about anything. Knew a fair bit about living off the country. Tracking things down.

And to me, he seemed to be okay ... for a white fella.

He took his time before he took me on, but I reckon he knew I'd be good money.

And he was right.

Saved his life once, I reckon. Up on Sweers Island in the Gulf. He'd gone up to try and help out when big sickness broke out there. Lots dead, others sick. Yeah, then he caught the sickness too. I nursed him lots, many, many days to get him back on his feet. He don't look a strong bloke ... slight, so to speak ... But a wiry type, plenty a fight in him.

He pulled through and he never forgot who helped him do so. Used to tell others of my great 'ministrations'.

There was plenty of things we shared and things he needed me to do. Now tracking is something that white fellas aren't that good at. And when you're moving big herds of horses or cattle, it comes in mighty handy. I tell you this ... there was very few stray animals we ever lost. Henry knew too that I'd find *him* if he ever got lost. Not that he did.

And what about those rivers? You'd get to these swollen, swirling rivers and you had to get horses and a whole lot of gear over to the other side. It meant swimming over and back a number of times to get the job done. One job took so long we built fires on both sides to warm up after each crossing. But we got everything, all our stock and all the gear.

That Henry's a great swimmer. Almost as good as me.

We went hundreds of miles together, moved stock, found new places, set up new stations. To me it felt a lot like we were good partners.

Then things went bust. All at once. I know it had to do with money and the banks. All we'd worked for was suddenly gone.

Now I don't drink but this was a bad time. Henry was away somewhere, and I ended up with a group ready to share their flask.

I was asleep when Henry returned.

He was angry with me, so angry he called me 'worthless'.

That was too much.

'Worthless?' I said. 'Worthless?'

I tugged my empty pockets.

'Here we are, boss,' I added. 'Lost all the stations, ten years in the bush, no money in the pocket.'

He went silent. Not a word. He walked away a little, then came back, his head bowed. He looked as if he'd lost all his strength.

'Ah well,' he said in a quiet voice, 'tomorrow more better you look out new fella master longa you.'

I had to think about that for a while. And there was really only one way to go.

I went over to where he was standing and asked, 'What time we startin' out tomorrow?'

Chapter 13

CATCHING CRIMINALS

FREDRIC URQUHART,
QUEENSLAND COMMISSIONER OF POLICE, 1919

'Catching criminals is hard enough when you're fully trained for it and backed up by other men,' Fredric Urquhart thought, 'but when you do it by yourself, it's even harder. Bordering on the lunatic.'

The Police Commissioner's mind was on the many memories he held of Ernest Henry.

Henry, he remembered, had never wanted to be a public servant. Even when he'd been acting as a warden on the Cloncurry gold fields.

Henry had once said to him – it was when Urquhart himself had been recovering in Cloncurry from a wound he had received from an Aboriginal and Henry had visited him, bringing books and conversation while Urquhart recuperated – Henry had told him, 'Just about every second person I know has been, is or is likely to be either a public servant or a Member of Parliament.'

'Look at old Dalrymple – Member for Kennedy and Colonial Secretary. And Sellheim, he did so well as Warden on the Gympie fields that Palmer, the Premier, has now promoted him to take charge of Charters Towers. I always thought that old Austrian baron would stay on the land. And even Sheaffe, now the Member for Burke in the State Legislature.'

Urquhart remonstrated with Henry.

'Henry,' he said, 'you've got to have public servants, you've got to have politicians. You've got to have order. Without the system 'twould be chaos.'

'Better than the chaos we have *with* the system?' Henry had chided.

Urquhart knew Henry's argument was half in jest, so he countered it, but lightly. Conversation was one of the things they both cherished. In this lonely, isolated region, which both travelled in considerable solitariness for much of the time. They treasured these occasions of conversation. Finding ways to come to terms with their environment, means of overcoming such solitude, was part of the challenge they both faced.

Both enjoyed reading. And Urquhart often found release, at the end of a busy period, in putting pen to paper and writing verse. It was something that Urquhart, in his later life, was to become reputed for. It was something he enjoyed but something he also disclaimed as a talent. Urquhart knew real verse and his, he said, did not measure up to any real standard. His family's history was not without note with one of his ancestors being credited with the translation of the *Rabelais* from French to English.

So, they continued their conversation, half in jest, about the merits and otherwise of the new colony's public service system. Yet, when the moment called for it, Henry had been ready to be a part of that system. The moments, however, were not ordinary occasions.

There was that time when, in the midst of criss-crossing the State and involving something like 3200 miles of horse-back riding, Henry had taken time out to become a law-enforcement officer.

It all started, as Urquhart recalled it, in late 1866 – after Henry's pastoralist failures and his move into prospecting. In the Cloncurry district, Henry and his partner, Roger Sheaffe, had discovered what they took to be a huge lode of ore of unusual weight and lustre. Not knowing what it was but eager to establish its identity and value, Henry loaded samples into his pack bags and set out for the nearest place where the find could be registered, and the material analysed. Henry's destination was Rockhampton, 800 miles away.

Henry, together with his blackboy, Dick, made his way east via Hughenden station which he had established but was now in the hands of his cousin, Robert Grey.

At Hughenden, the station's overseer had been shot in the chest – the result of a squabble when the station overseer had refused to lend a horse to one of the station's workers, a man named O'Dowd. Henry's cousin, Gray, was away from the station at the time. So Henry, having established which way the offender had headed, advised those at the station, including the local magistrate, that he would 'keep an eye out' for the man who seemed to have gone in the direction Henry intended travelling. In fact, Henry had been appalled by the criminal behaviour of O'Dowd and would make it his business to capture the man, if that was possible.

Sworn in as a special constable by a local squatter who was also a magistrate, and armed with a warrant, Henry moved on. Henry then started out for the Peak Downs copper mine, some 350 miles away. He took with him two blocks of the minerals he had brought with him for assay. Each, weighing 50 lb a piece, were secured in his saddle bags.

Along the way to Peak Downs he continued to make enquiries about the assailant. Finally, he heard of a man answering O'Dowd's description working at Bowen Downs station. The name the man had given, however, was Kennedy.

With one of the station's overseers, he went to where the man was shepherding at an outstation. Henry wasn't sure how he would identify the man, so he took the direct approach. As he rode up to the man he called out, as though he had recognised the man, 'Your name is O'Dowd.' The man answered 'Yes.' And Henry had him. He showed the man the warrant he bore with him from Hughenden.

With Henry's 'official' approach and the waving of the warrant, O'Dowd took Henry to be a bona fide constable. O'Dowd offered no resistance and asked that Henry not handcuff him. Henry, in fact, had no handcuffs to do so. Not that he let the villain know that.

Henry, therefore, acceded to the man's request but realised he needed some way to keep the man secure of a night until he could deliver him to the proper authorities. So, Henry bought a dog chain and a padlock at the station. At night he locked one end of the dog chain to O'Dowd's ankle and fastened the other end around his own left wrist. Henry made the man sleep at the length of the chain from him. In that way, O'Dowd could not move without awakening Henry.

Henry told me he slept at night with his clothes on and his revolver in his belt.

Another thing in Henry's favour was that the desperado was a poor horseman. So, there was little chance he could make a dash for his freedom during the journey.

It wasn't too long, however, until the outlaw woke up to the fact that Henry was not a constable. O'Dowd then tried to employ delaying tactics, slowing down his horse. Henry wasn't having any of this. He waited until O'Dowd caught up with him and Henry told him that he would have to keep up with Henry.

When O'Dowd refused, Henry's temper gave way. He broke a thick branch off a tree, stripped it and told O'Dowd he was, indeed, taking the villain in to justice. With that, he started O'Dowd's horse into a gallop and ran it for a mile with O'Dowd hanging on for grim life.

'The next time I have to use the branch,' he told O'Dowd, 'it won't be on the horse. It will be over your head.'

That settled the matter and Henry delivered his prisoner to the nearest police station, Clermont, 280 miles away.

Then Henry continued his journey to Rockhampton where analysis of the rock he carried showed that it was iron, not copper. For many a man this might have proved to be an insurmountable disappointment. Not so to Henry. He was to return to the Cloncurry area, find another outcrop and travel the same route again the have the rock analysed – this time successfully. But that was another story.

'I don't think I'd like to be a public servant,' Henry had told Urquhart. 'Too much report writing, too much stuck behind a desk.'

Urquhart knew just what Henry was talking about. For, although a public servant himself, it was the action of the job that he really enjoyed.

Urquhart was certain, however, that had fate dictated a public service career for Henry, then Henry would have made a fine police officer. Maybe, even, a fine police commissioner.

Chapter 14

COHABITATION

ROBERT GRAY,
COUSIN OF ERNEST HENRY
1867

I'm sorry I missed Ernest on his way through last year. We have a lot of catching up to do since I took over Hughenden.

Henry's chasing down the criminal was a concern to me. Not that it came as a surprise. It wasn't the first time he had done something like that.

It was before Ernest came up the Hughenden. He and I and a gentleman named Bell were in Bowen staying in a hotel. When we got up in the morning, we found each of our horses were gone from the hotel's stables.

At that time, too, there were no police around. So, Ernest and the landlord had themselves sworn in as special constables and took off after the horse thieves. The chase covered about 100 miles before they caught up with the thieves. They captured the culprits and brought the felons, and the horses, back to Bowen.

But I am concerned for my cousin. His loss of all the industry he built up – all the stations he established throughout Queensland. It has driven him to the outer edge, out to the farthest frontier.

I know he fears no man – black or white. At least around here there are other white men to associate with, even if some of them are crooks. But, out where he is, he has just himself to count on. One man among a lot of blacks. Savages, some of them.

I know that Ernest takes care of his dealings with the natives. They are, he says, like children. Love to joke, like to laugh. And Ernest can see in them what many can't – an ingenuity and intelligence. He has a way of working with them, of building up a trust that many can't or won't.

Some won't tolerate them. Others fear them. Others would as soon shoot them as say hello. They won't feel safe until there's no native left within rifle shot of them. Wipe them out is the way they feel.

Henry left here for Coppertown to have his mineral lode assayed. I know from the route he took that he is likely to pass through one of my new neighbour's property and I hope he has had the chance to meet Robert Christison. I think they'd have a lot to talk about.

Christison is the son of a parish minister in England. He has taken up his Lammermoor run some 50 miles out of Hughenden. The 'Meenister's son', as he sometimes describes himself, is the sixth of seven children and he has known scarcity in his childhood. He had made a vow to himself that one day he would own more land than his master in the old country. And in that he certainly succeeded.

But when he took up his run, he built his homestead on the main watercourse within the property and took a deliberate long-term decision that, rather than banishing the original inhabitants of the area, he would accommodate them.

To do this, he first had to talk to them. And to do that, he needed to have a native who understood what he said.

His solution to this was to capture one of the local natives and hold him as long as it took for the native to learn English and for Christison to learn the local language. He not only achieved this but also built up trust and even a friendship with the native.

The native, who Christison named 'Barney' proved most intelligent.

'He picked up English much quicker than I could pick up his language,' Christison told me.

'Barney' became Christison's emissary to 'Barney's' tribe, the Dalleburra. Christison's message was simple.

Christison undertook not to harm the Dalleburra but the tribe was not to harm Christison or Christison's people. The tribe could camp on the far side of the waterhole and kill native animals. But they were not to kill horses or sheep. Christison told 'Barney' to invite the Dalleburra people to come back to him when they wanted to talk. They were to come without weapons. They were to come in peace.

Some days later, signal smoke arose throughout the tribal areas and the natives gathered on the far side of the waterhole. They came in family groups with wives and children. But they also came armed with clubs, boomerangs and long spears.

Christison, by himself, rode down to the other side of the waterhole, wondering if he would live to see the sunset. But, one by one, and led by 'Barney', the blacks swam across the water to meet and greet Christison.

There was great celebration that lasted into the night when

Christison retired to his hut. He noticed in the next few days that, while some of the blacks wandered off to their lands to hunt, others remained around the waterhole doing not much fishing and even less hunting.

His suspicions were reinforced when 'Barney' came to him, warning him not to sleep in the hut that night.

'I was happy because I knew there would come a time when I had to re-enforce the policy and, the sooner the better as far as I was concerned,' Christison told me.

He waited, that night, secreted up a tree near his locked hut. He had with him his double-barrelled shotgun loaded with buckshot. When the stealthy natives snuck to the door and rattled it, Christison loosed the shots. In profound fright and bearing the imprints of the blast, the natives fled into the night.

The next day Christison went to the camp, singled out the offenders and admonished them soundly. It was the last time that there was any infringement of the agreement between Christison and the Dalleburra.

Chapter 15

A HILL OF COPPER

ERNEST HENRY

I clenched my battle axe – in reality, it was a tomahawk – and shouted to the lonesome winds: 'There is a tide in the affairs of men which, taken at the flood, leads on to fortune'.

Shakespeare in the Spinifex. My thoughts were vaulting, higher than the limitless sky that rode above.

It was copper. A hill of copper. A 50-foot-high hill. All copper.

Well, it would have to be tested, of course, but I knew it was copper. This was not going to be a false start like the earlier one which turned out to be iron. I had learned a lot since I'd been to Peak Downs where I had visited with the first hopeful consignment of metal. At Peak Downs I had learned how to distinguish the true signs of copper.

It was May 1867, less than a year since our first trip for the fruitless assay. Now I knew what to look for, and I had found it.

Dick and I had returned to the northwest and, on that day, there was just he and I in that vast territory. There was no other white man within 100 miles of where we stood. We were in the vicinity of where the town of Cloncurry would later grow.

Dick, as he always did, had brought up the horses that morning and we had breakfast. Then it was time for exploring. I left Dick to look after the camp. I made sure he had plenty of firearms to protect himself if the blacks came around the camp.

I intended being thorough in my search for any copper. At every lode or vein of rock I came across, when riding in the hills, I dismounted and used my tomahawk to break the rock, using the blunt side of the axe.

The first trace I came across was in a slate formation rock. There were no outward indications of copper, but I got a great satisfaction when a blow to the rock revealed its presence. Although I failed to trace the vein any distance, the siting gave me the confidence to carry on. I found nothing of significance for the rest of the day and nor on the second day of searching.

On day three, I circled the hills around the spot where I found the first indications. I covered a good many miles and searched a multitude of rocks and ridges from sunrise until late afternoon. I had found not even a trace of copper.

I was working my way back towards the camp when I came upon some loose fragments of tolerably rich ore. I immediately dismounted and tried to find a vein. Leading my horse, I found, here and there, pieces of ore. I tied up the horse so that I could move about more freely.

Following the indications with my eyes intent on the ground and my faculties alert with expectation and anticipation, I was led to a rock, standing seven or eight feet above the ground, one side of which was covered with green copper stains.

After examining it and feeling that I was drawing near to some great discovery, for the first time since leaving my horse, I raised my eyes to look around and, lo, not 100 yards from me was a rocky hill, about 50 feet in height, carrying copper stains to its very summit. I closed my eyes and opened them again to be sure it was not an illusion, then walked over and climbed the hill – an immense outcrop of copper ore. It was a realisation and far more, of my convictions.

What might it not mean for me, I thought.

It was a supreme moment, that of satisfaction and triumph. What thoughts flashed through my mind, of my past troubles and losses; subsequent struggles; my journey, the year before, to Peak Downs ending in disappointment.

I had not time, on the evening of my great discovery, to do more than convince myself of the existence of masses of rich ore lying on the surface. But the next day we shifted our camp up to the copper outcrop, so I might have plenty of time to give it a thorough inspection.

After some time thus employed, I rode to the northward, the direction in which the lode bears, to see if it extended further on. A few hundred yards brought me on to a level plain, traversing which for about two miles I ascended a low ridge on the crown of which was another large vein with blocks of ore lying scattered along it. On breaking one of the latter, the cleavage revealed several nodules of pure copper.

Not being then aware that it had ever before been found in a virgin state, you may imagine my elation.

On returning to camp, I found Dick had been amusing himself by breaking up a vein of yellow jasper which proved to be studded within with small specks of pure copper but which he took to be gold.

I now felt sure there must be much larger specimens to be found on the main outcrop, so, having other work to attend to, I told Dick to take his tomahawk and knock about amongst the ore till he found some copper nuggets the size of his fist. In about an hour he returned, jubilant, with his pockets full and said, as he emptied them of pure metal, 'Talk about copper mines, look at that.' Some pieces were as big as his fist.

'Now Dick,' I said, 'I'm going to find a lump as big as my head,' and sure enough did so.

The finds, which were subsequently proven to be copper, were the foundation for what became the Great Australia Mine.

Chapter 16

DEATH IN THE BUSH

MARIAN HENRY, ERNEST'S WIFE, 1881

When I asked Ernest why he fell in love with me, he said it was because I was such a fearless horsewoman.

'Not only that, but anything a horse can pull, you can drive,' he advised me. 'In this country, that makes you invaluable.'

Then he smiled and gave me a gentle hug.

I wrote on my slate, 'And I thought it was because I was so good at bookkeeping.'

Bookkeeping was something that I had learned well from my father who was a bank manager. He also taught me how to ride.

I told Ernest, more than once, that I suspected my being a mute had also been an attraction for him.

I knew that he'd lived so long by himself, almost a hermit, that quiet and solitude was probably something he cherished by now.

And conversing with me by writing – it may have been a difficulty for some men, but Ernest was an inveterate writer – almost every week he would pen a letter to his mother or father.

This was something I was also good at – writing. And it gave me great pleasure and satisfaction to help him in his correspondence, not just to his family but also in business matters. I would write the letters and show them to Ernest before he would sign them and send them on their way – whenever we could catch the post, which was not only erratic but infrequent in the northwest.

My bookkeeping skills were equally applied to his assistance. In part, that meant helping Ernest with the operation of his stores at Boulia and Cloncurry.

For, while Henry continued to explore for copper and discover some amazing finds, he and I both knew it may be some time before circumstances made the working or sale of these finds economically possible. Opening the stores was a means to keeping financially afloat until we could realise upon the copper finds.

So, while I did not attend the counter in the stores, I worked on the accounting side to register the receipt and sales of the items the store stocked. We sold everything from hats to horseshoes. Whenever we could get them. Ordering goods in itself could take months. Getting the goods forwarded to us could take just as long again.

Almost everything we got came all the way from Brisbane. The goods were landed at the Norman River, at the town of Normanton. Then they came overland to Cloncurry.

The costs were exorbitant. Fruit came mostly in tins. And, for example, California peaches sold for more than five shillings a tin.

Jam was three shillings a tin. Dried apples came delivered in barrels. Dried potatoes were in tins.

I never really got a chance to show Ernest that I could cook. I never had the opportunity to try out the many recipes I had inherited from my mother. The spirit was willing, but the ingredients were nowhere to be found.

You are far from anyone here in that harsh yet handsome country. I am a country rather than a city girl, but the vast distances of Queensland amaze me. Have amazed me since the time we first came here after we married.

To get to the north we came by steamer – the *Black Swan* – from Brisbane to Townsville. Townsville was then the most northerly port on the northern coast.

Henry told me the story of how Townsville had come to be established not long before we sailed for there. It was founded because of an argument.

It would appear that a Mr John Black, who was then the superintendent of the northern region Woodstock Station, worked for Robert Towns & Co of Sydney, one of the major pioneers of projects in the north.

As Henry told the story, Black disagreed with one of the forwarding agents at Bowen which was then the only port in those waters. The agent was dictating the rates of carriage from the port to Towns' Burdekin properties.

Black took umbrage at the agent's unyielding stance. He warned the agent that he would pay for that stance.

'There is a creek entering the sea to the northward that is much nearer to Woodstock than Bowen and I shall advise Captain Towns to send his schooner up there with our next landing,' Black told the Bowen agent.

And the outcome was that Towns did as Black advised and this saw the opening of a new port to later become known as Townsville, built on a creek which was Ross River. Townsville has got off to a good start and only time will tell which port, Townsville or Bowen, will become the main produce handler in northern Queensland.

In Townsville, Ernest purchased a buckboard and horses and we proceeded from there by overland track to Cloncurry, 500 miles inland. We travelled by way of the Dalrymple Crossing of the Burdekin, thence via the Cape River diggings to Hughenden Station and Richmond Downs.

In all that great distance there was just the one hostelry, at Dalrymple Crossing.

It was a comfortable low-roofed building of slabs and shingles. It stood in a sheltered bend on the western side of the wide, sandy river channel shaded by white-boled gums.

We also rested a few days at Hughenden Station, the property that Ernest had originally established and now the home of his cousin Robert Gray. From there we pushed on across the extensive Mitchell-grass plains to Cloncurry. In fact, there was no township there when Ernest erected our first home. It had a chimney of rubble stone, cemented together with ant-bed and built into a natural cairn of rocks with bloodwood forks for uprights and with saplings laid across for wall-plates. Ernest formed the building, sheeting it with slabs of bark, and with cane-grass he thatched the roof.

It was humble. It was rustic. But it was our home. I was part of a new landscape which, while harsh in many ways, held its own discernible character and charm.

A panorama of untamed wilderness extended from our front door. The ranges rose from beyond the river to the south-west. I noticed, quite regularly, the smoke in these ranges. Part of the native method of hunting included the burning of Spinifex grass to flush out animals.

The hills and mountains are cut from stones, and they protrude heavenward at chiselled angles. In the chill winter those forms and their colours command the eye. In summer they shimmer in a haze that is hard to bear. Yet even then, in all that heat, the colours arrayed within the metal walls they present are so deep and distinctive at sunrise and sunset that, as Ernest says, it makes you feel a master painter has been at work.

The heat and other difficulties, I feel, took their toll on me. And on the children too. And Ernest broached the subject of my returning to Warwick and taking the children with me. We discussed this at length. I did not wish to leave him there alone. But he prevailed upon me to make the move and now we await visits from him whenever he can leave the copper country.

The one thing I did miss most of all, during my time in Cloncurry, was the companionship of other women. When we were married, I believe, I was the first woman to come to these parts. There are still few there.

Among those who settled there, Mrs Alexander Kennedy. Ernest first met Kennedy back when he was opening the store in Boulia. And so, we – myself and Mrs Kennedy – became acquainted during my time there.

Mrs Kennedy was fortunate in a way that I was not. Her husband, together with a Mr Curry, ran the properties they held in that country. And Mrs Kennedy's sister was married to Mr Curry. So, the two ladies had each other for company and enjoyed that happy circumstance very much.

In a recent sad letter for Ernest, he informed me that their property,

Noranside on the Burke River, had been sold and, because the older children needed to be educated, they decided to go to the nearest school – at Normanton.

To get there, the women, who felt they were in need of a change from station life, set out for Cloncurry. There was Mr and Mrs Kennedy and their three children and the Curries with their three. The men rode out on horses. The women and children travelled in a spring-cart and horse-dray.

What started out as a much-anticipated adventure changed abruptly with the onset of an early monsoon deluge. The bush paths became bogs. The party made its way as far as Rocky Waterhole near Chatsworth Station. But they could go no further because of the swollen streams.

So, they decided to camp and wait out the rain. They made themselves comfortable in their pitched tents, but the rain went on for days. They could go nowhere.

And, amidst all this, Mrs Curry, who was expecting, gave birth in that roadside tent.

Mrs Curry was struck down with dysentery. So, too, were her infant, her second youngest child, and Mrs Kennedy's youngest child. They were caught in the midst of the floods and the rains with no proper nourishment and without medicines.

Mrs Currie and her two sons died there. But the baby and Mrs Kennedy's sick child survived thanks to the milk provided by a pony that had just foaled.

They buried Mrs Currie and her children on the spot.

I grieve for them all but most keenly for Mrs Kennedy.

Chapter 17

RIGHTING A RIOT

Marian Henry, wife of Ernest Henry

1880

If a man is in a position of authority, he must look the part. Particularly if he is going out to quell a riot.

At the very least, he has to look the best he can.

That's what I told my Ernest. Well, not in words as, from birth, I have been deaf and, consequently, mute. But Ernest and I have learned to communicate.

The message arrived at night. They wanted Ernest, as acting warden on the Cloncurry gold fields, to come and solve a major disagreement on the Top Camp diggings situated among the rugged nearby ranges. It was a remarkable field with the gold gained there as pure as any found anywhere in Australia.

Well, it was more than a disagreement. Armed bands of white diggers fighting crowds of Chinese miners. One dead. Many injured.

Such a dear, sweet man is my Ernest. But fearless too.

It was just that, as he hurried towards the hut door early the next morning dressed for all the world like a miner himself – which, when you think of it, he is – well, I had to pull him up.

It was because of his minerals expertise that the government had asked him to be the local mining warden. It was one of the most remote corners of Queensland and, since there was no one else available, he accepted the position.

Being so far from anywhere, it's not the place where you dress up a lot. So, Henry did not carry an extensive wardrobe. But his one white shirt I held out to him. Once that was on, I gave him his set of braces for his trousers. And then I fitted him out with a clean handkerchief for his shirt pocket.

By the time Ernest arrived at the diggings, some 400 miners, white and yellow and both with truculent dispositions, were marshalled there. There was just Ernest to dispense British law.

His main aim was to find a settlement satisfactory to both. And that, he decided, meant separating the two groups.

At first, he offered them alternate claims on the same field, but they equally disagreed. Finally, he found an area where just two claims had been lodged by white men and it was this area that he made available to the Chinese diggers providing those claims were relinquished. The Chinamen and the whites accepted this and, almost immediately the Chinese moved to their new area of work. In time, the Chinese found their new field to be as lucrative and the areas they had left.

Chapter 18
BIG FELLA COPPER

ERNEST HENRY, 1882

I met Tubbie Terrier about two years ago, towards the end of 1880, while exploring an unknown tract of land on the Upper Dugald River.

That wasn't his real name, his Kalkadoon name. But it was as close as I could get to pronouncing it. So, Tubbie Terrier it is.

Meeting Tubbie was to lead to yet another major copper discovery.

At the time, I remember writing to my wife, Marian – who was then living in Warwick with our children – I still had the copper exploration all to myself in the area.

'So,' I told her, 'I had better make hay while the sun shines.'

I had a dray, loaded with camp gear and six weeks' rations and took with me two of my blackboys, Dan and Joe. Joe's gin, Fanny, also came with me. And James Young.

James was looking for gold. A veteran fossicker, he had no interest in copper whatsoever. However, we had known each other a while and got on well together and it was always good to have his company along in those lonely ranges.

The area we were scouring was on the Upper Dugald River which forms the watershed between the Leichardt and Cloncurry Rivers that feed into the Gulf.

I got the inclination to go there as my friend, Roger Sheaffe, some years earlier, had discovered an ingot of native copper on the Dugald. The 8-cwt nugget was loaded into a dray and taken to Normanton and, from there to the smelters. But no larger amount of copper was found in the near vicinity. Nevertheless, it sounded to me like a good place to start looking for a lode.

Leaving from Granada Station, we entered the wilderness country and proceeded up the Dugald valley where we found squibs of copper. It was a land of rocky soil showing just Spinifex and small mountain gums, more a shrub than a tree. There were the occasional bloodwoods and turpentine bushes and, now and then, a desert gum noted for its beautiful scent.

It is a land of dramatic shapes. Peaked mountains, razor backs and toothed ridges, narrow and saw-blades and the central mass itself of ranges with granite spires. From up there, at the top of the Upper Dugald, vast plains and level scrublands sweep away and provide the country through which so many watercourses head towards the Gulf.

The countryside itself changes with the time of day. By noon, the burning sun has bleached much of the vibrant colour of the landscape which regains its rainbow hues at either sundown or sun-up. By night, the overhead sky is a showcase of diamonds.

We formed a camp on Cabbage Tree Creek and there I left Jim in charge of the dray while my blackboy, Joe, and I pushed on into the mass of broken ranges upward toward the watershed. I took Joe, a Mittakoodi from the Williams River country with me as he assured me that he spoke the language of the Kalkadoons who lived in these hills.

In this country there was evidence of local natives hunting. We had seen smoke coming from the ranges. Firing the Spinifex grass was a method that the aboriginals used in hunting.

We made camp and the next day pushed on up into the ranges. The country was so gruelling that I was considering heading back down. But suddenly, we heard voices from the range above us. We rode on, upwards, to a small plateau. Joe's horse was somewhat distressed, so he had dismounted and was leading his horse a short way behind my progress.

We found the black camp in a small depression almost on the top of the range. There were a few wurlies thatched with Spinifex. There were only women and piccaninnies in the camp. As I approached on horseback, the children ran off to hide in among rocks. The gins, too, were alarmed.

But they became reassured when Joe appeared. He told them not to be afraid of me and assured them that the horses would not bite or eat them.

An elderly gin spoke with Joe and said she would go to look for the men who were hunting.

She didn't go far but mounted a rock eminence near the camp overhanging a network of gullies that hemmed the foot of the plateau. From its summit she sent out a call, a piercing note, beginning in the bass and running up in perfect scale to a flute-like note. When the highest crescendo had been reached, the call was suddenly cut off with the result that the flute-like echo could be heard floating far in the surrounding hills.

Soon the Kalkadoon warriors began to come in.

Among them was Tubbie, a tall, athletic figure of a man, standing over six feet tall. I put his age to be in his early twenties. He could well have looked fierce, had he intended to do so, but, in fact, his countenance was that of a kindly person. He was, he told Joe, a member of the big hill tribe.

I noted one peculiarity about the man. He was perfectly webbed between all ten toes.

We – I through Joe – spoke with Tubbie for some length of time and we invited him back to our camp at Cabbage Tree Creek where we had left the dray. The natives were very much in favour of this. They said they would be there the next day. They arrived, in fact, five days later. It wasn't the full party, just Tubbie, his gin and another blackfellow with his gin.

Together with Joe, I took Tubbie and his fellow blackfellow to a nearby spot where there were strains of green carbonate of copper showing in slate. I asked Tubbie if he knew where such metal occurred in large amounts.

He replied, 'Yes, plenty, all about, big fella.'

In exchange for a tomahawk and some old clothing, Tubbie agreed to take me to a spot where 'big fella copper sat down.'

We were in an exceedingly good mood and that night we all sat down around the campfire. On such occasions, I enjoy a good song and I sang many of those I'd learned in my sailor apprenticeship days.

I don't think they knew what the shanties were about unless Joe might have provided them with a rough translation later on.

In any case, they seemed to like the singing, and, in fact, I heard one of the gins humming one of the tunes the next day.

We left that same day to find the copper. Myself, Joe and the four

Kalkadoons. We – Joe and I – went on horseback. The blacks on foot. But it was they who, bounding along, set the pace, leaping over rocks and clumps of Spinifex. Tubbie, in fact, was disconcerted that we, on horses, were going too slow. We covered some 15 miles up Cabbage Tree Creek that day.

Tubbie showed us, during this expedition, a landscape featuring ravines, waterfalls, and hidden hideaways of polished granite. And springs of pure water emanating from sandstone walls. He was showing us the secret country of his countrymen.

The next day we proceeded up the creek for 10 miles to its head and came, among the ranges to a watercourse bearing westerly. It was here that Tubbie advised us that the rest of the journey would be too tough for horses. We hobbled the horses and left them, together with equipment, with the two gins and the remainder of our party proceeded the last three miles of our journey over extremely rough, rocky country.

The soles of my boots were all but worn out and I felt, most severely, the sharp rocks and Spinifex tufts that marked our way. The barefoot blacks, however, showed little intention of easing the pace at which they travelled.

I think the expedition must have sapped not just my strength but also my spirit a little. It was as tough a going as I've experience anywhere in my long travels throughout various parts of this huge country. And I must admit I was not greatly hopeful, at that moment, of any major find.

I was, therefore, totally amazed and astonished as I beheld what we came upon – a range crest and the huge quartz reef that ran along it. The reef presented the most imposing outcrop of copper ore, 50 feet high in one spot and unbroken along a length of 130 feet and with formations that spread along the crest for over a mile.

The natives called it Yamamillah. Or shortened it to 'armilla'. To me, it became Argylla, one of Australia's greatest ever copper discoveries.

Chapter 19

WARFARE

Tubbie Terrier, 1920

I remember this man, Henry. A big fella. Bit skinny. White beard.
Met him first about 50 years ago. Up in the mountains. Him and
his Mittakoodi. Fella named Joe, I think. The day I was out hunting,
me, Kuda, and other members of our mob.

And Henry, he could sing. Yeah, he could sing. Won't ever forget
that night and that voice of his echoing around the mountains as we
all sat down by the campfire. Gave me some things if I'd take him to
the copper.

Wouldn't do that now. Not now I know what I do.

He and his mates, they ended up with everything. Us Kalkadoons,
we got nothing.

Don't mean I don't like him. As a man. He was, I reckon, a good man. Leastwise his Mitakoodi, Joe, said so. And the other Mitakoodis with him. And I reckoned so, too. He was a man I thought you could trust.

Truth was, you can't trust any of them. They wanted everything that was ours. And they took it.

You got to know, they're all not exactly the same. Some would soon as shoot you on sight. 'Only good abbo,' they'd say, 'is a dead one.' Others would try to get on with the Kalkadoons. No trouble as long as we gave them no trouble. 'Don't go spearing our cattle or we'll come get you.'

Henry, I guess, he was more like the second mob. First up, he didn't bring cattle with him. And I never knew of him to shoot at a blackfella. Lots of ducks and birds and kangaroos, but not at a blackfella. But, at the end of the day, he was white, and he lived by the white man's ways and laws. He was friends with those who chased us from our land.

One way or another, there was always going to be a war. They wanted our land; they wanted our water. We couldn't live without either.

Them cattle and horses. They didn't just drink the water. They'd shit and piss in it. Made it no use for us afterwards. And they'd trample down the grass and wreck the plants and berries we used to eat. What you going to do if you're starving and dying of thirst. And we lost our sacred sites. Like, say, someone coming and burning down all the white fellas' churches.

We were losing our homes, our water, and our food. And we also lost our women when whites would come and take them away.

You can't live like that. Except as their slaves. And the Kalkadoons were never born to be slaves.

We lived in our castles, the mountains. And since long before any white man came here with his cattle that drank and fouled our creeks and rivers, the Kalkadoons had fought to keep this land our own. Other tribes knew to fear the Kalkadoons. The Mitakoodi, the Pitta Pitta and others.

And the white man knew they had a fight on their hands with us. We had the weapons; we had the mountain hideaways. And we showed them they could not just come in and steal what was ours. We ambushed them where we could. We kept them bottled up on their properties. And when they sent out their police, we took care of that, too.

The white people, they got really scared when some of our mob killed Beresford back in '83. Him and some of his native troopers. Silly bugger didn't know our men could put their hands on weapons when he herded them into that ravine. Thought they were safely tucked up. But they got their weapons and fell on the troopers and broke out.

Beresford, he was police. And police were the people who spoke for the whole of the white people. The chief of these people was far, far away. No Kalkadoon ever met or saw them. I think, probably, that neither had many of the white people themselves.

But, because this chief said so, our lands – the land of the Kalkadoons, and those of all other tribes – were now 'Crown' lands. And the chiefs could give that land away to any one they liked. And if we didn't like it, the chiefs would send their police to show us we had to give away our land. The white chiefs had no time for us, no time for the 'niggers' – the cards were all stacked in the white man's favour.

I think many of them were shocked when we fought back.

Things changed when the police sent that man, Urquhart. I tell you, before he got there that town was full of fright. Even the native troopers were useless. Just hanging around town, huddled in with the whites.

Urquhart, and his big horse Hamlet, arrived and changed all that. He got his blacks out of the town, out to a camp north of Cloncurry. Flat country on a camp. And he made them practice – riding, shooting, tracking and drill, drill, drill. By the time he was finished with them, them black troopers were ready to go out and do more killing.

It was 1884, as I remember. And later that year was a big fight. It was a bloke called Powell and he was a partner of Kennedy. Powell was moving cattle and he decided to use a waterhole that the Kalkadoons had always used. Powell shooed the black men away and took his cattle to the water to drink.

That night, the men attacked Powell's camp. They were frightened that Powell might be waiting, with his guns, for the attack. His 'boy' had got wind of the attack and had warned Powell but the white man decided not to take the advice. He went to sleep instead.

When Kennedy and other whites in the area heard of this fight they got together with Urquhart and his troopers, and they tracked down the Kalkadoons responsible. When they found them, they killed them.

The big fight was later that year. Battle Mountain. That's what the whites call it today when they talk about it.

They gathered together in great numbers with their guns – revolvers and rifles – the police under Urquhart, the graziers mustered by Hopkins of Granada where, it was said, a Chinese shepherd had been murdered. And all the station hands. And their horses thundered towards us; we were there, myself and Kuda among a great horde of Kalkadoons. We were armed with our spears and *nulla-nullas*. And we were ready for them. From high within our country, we could see the wild men driving towards us. The messages went out for the warriors to come. We did, and we chose the battle ground. Battle Mountain, as they now call it.

By now we knew about the power of revolvers and rifles. The .577 Sniders were the police rifles. There may have also been some of the breech-loader Martini-Henrys. Both of them could kill you far beyond a spear's throw distance. We had our wooden spears. We had our wooden clubs. And we had the mountains. Sheer on one side and defendable from the plains from which the mounted men were racing towards us.

We knew the mountain would make the horses useless. It was too steep, and the riders had to dismount to make their scramble up the slope. It was so steep they had to come scrambling up on hands and knees. We were up on a ridge above them, and we sent down a rain of spears and stone and rocks. Their rifles were dangerous, when they could get to use them, but we hid behind giant anthills.

I stood with Kuda, and we were in the first line of the battle. Closest to the police who were leading the attackers. We both saw that the police chief – his name was Urquhart – was leading the attack up the hill.

Kuda saw a chance to stop Urquhart and probably, then, the white men's attack. He slipped down the hill and hid behind a large anthill in the path that Urquhart was making towards the top.

When Urquhart was almost upon him, Kuda stepped into Urquhart's way and tossed a large slab of broken anthill at him. It hit Urquhart in the head – smashing into the big policeman's face. He dropped to the ground and Kuda, now picking up his club, raced forward to finish the man.

But a bullet from a Native Police rifle felled Kuda. I stood up to run to help Kuda. There was another rifle shot. It grazed my head and I fell next to him, unconscious but still alive.

It was later in the day when I came round. All that was left were bodies – Kalkadoon warriors – spread along the slopes on which I lay. My head was bloody and ached and I soon fell back into unconsciousness. When I awoke, it was late at night. There was little moonlight, and I made my way slowly towards where Kuda had fallen. He was lifeless, like so many other of my brothers. I crawled off the mountain, more dead than alive and hid in the wilderness, away from the search parties of Native Police who patrolled the area for days afterwards.

I wanted, most of all, to get back to my wife who I had left when we went to join the tribe. But first I had to regain my strength. For days I hid in a thick grove of trees near a waterhole and went at night to drink at the creek. Gradually my body began to recover but I was filled with the sorrow and the memories of the many men who had fallen beside their spears.

I did, finally, reach my woman and she was waiting, as we left them, with Kuda's wife. No one was left to care for Kuda's woman so now I took her, too, as my wife, and we all fled to find somewhere to live.

It was many weeks later that we came to a station where, we had heard, we might find some safety. It was a station owned by a man named MacDonald. Others of the tribe knew him as a person who was fair to Kalkadoons.

We, us three, made our way slowly onto the station. We were met by a 'blackboy' who told us to stop while he went back to the homestead to speak with the 'Boss'. We waited, tired, thirsty and almost starving, very anxious about what might happen to us.

Eventually the 'blackboy' returned on horseback and beckoned to us. He asked us to sit down then unloaded both food and drink from his pack which he gave to us.

We had found our shelter. And, later, when the Native Police came looking for Battle Mountain 'stragglers', MacDonald told them there were none on his station and the Native Police left.

It was here, on MacDonald's run, that I stayed, in safety and respect, long after the Native Police faded away and Battle Mountain was just a memory to a dwindling number of men, black and white.

Chapter 20

POWELL

Fredric C. Urquhart

Queensland Commissioner of Police

1919

1884 was the year it all happened. And James Powell's murder in July that year was one of the turning points.

I was twenty-nine years old. I'd been an officer in the Queensland Native Mounted Police for a little over two years. I'd been in the Cloncurry district for just four months.

Things were chaotic when I got there.

A year earlier Sub-Inspector Beresford, my predecessor, had been killed by the Kalkadoons. He thought he had them bottled up – captured – in a gorge up at the head of the Williams River. But they were in their own territory. He had herded them into an area where, unbeknown to him, they had a hidden cache of weapons. And at night they attacked. Slaughtered him and nearly all his black troopers. Their rocky graves mark that desolated spot where they died.

Then the blacks ran riot. Spearing cattle, threatening properties and the township itself. You couldn't go anywhere unarmed. The town itself, stuck out hundreds of miles from anywhere, thought the natives were going to launch an all-out attack. Emboldened, the savages even issued challenges to the townspeople to 'come out and fight' and meet the same fate as Beresford.

Alexander Kennedy from Calton Downs went to Brisbane to demand the government send aid.

And that's how I was posted there. Sub-Inspector Frederick Urquhart, under instructions from Seymour, the Police Commissioner himself, to break the Kalkadoon threat. And to pay special attention to Kennedy's area.

And Powell, the man who the Kalkadoons had now killed, was Kennedy's partner at Calton Downs.

Not an auspicious start. But things could, I suppose, have been worse. A few months earlier, when I first arrived in Cloncurry, the local black mounted troopers were in a woefully bad shape, afraid for their own lives from the Kalkadoon threat. And there were no horses. They'd all disappeared when Beresford was slain.

The few months grace I had been given gave me time to regroup. To get the horses and other supplies I needed to patrol this vast area. A time to get intelligence I needed from people such as Kennedy himself and from the experienced local prospector, Ernest Henry. And, most important, to get my troopers retrained out at our camp on the Corella River some 25 miles north of the town. There we trained, on foot, on horse and till our riding, our hunting and our shooting skills were what we needed.

We – myself and six troopers - were ready to ride by 9 am the day after we received word of the attack on Powell. We had just completed the loading of the large quantity of rations we required when Kennedy rode into Cloncurry to join us.

And then we were off, heading into Kalkadoon territory.

By the next day we were at McDonald's on Cameron Creek. It was here we took on Jacky, Powell's blackboy.

'I warn 'em, warn 'em Boss,' Jacky told us. 'He not listen.'

Jacky had snapped awake the night of the attack by Powell's warning shouts. He saw Powell speared by the band of attackers and took a spear wound himself. While the savages concentrated on bludgeoning Powell, Jacky had managed to slip away into the bush. He made a painful trek to the nearest station where he raised the alarm.

Jacky told me that Powell and he were driving straggling cattle from Kamilaroi. The blackboy added that, when a few miles from the scene of the massacre, at dinner time they met the blacks who appeared very friendly. Mr Powell gave them bread and meat and a lot of tobacco and two of them stayed with them to help them drive the cattle through some rough gorges during the afternoon.

It appears that the remainder of the mob must have followed on behind and watched Mr Powell's camp through the night. Jacky said that about three hours before daylight he was awakened by hearing Mr Powell call out, 'Look out, Jack.' The blackboy jumped up and saw Mr Powell surrounded by blacks. Powell had a revolver in his hand which would not go off.

Jacky bolted off into the bush, receiving a spear in the back as he did so. He subsequently looked back from some rising ground and saw blacks dancing round the campfire and heard them beating the body of Mr Powell with clubs. He then travelled as fast as he could to the station which he reached on the third day. An examination of the tracks showed that the blacks followed the boy a considerable distance but for some reason abandoned the pursuit.

We took Jacky with us on that ride to find the slain Powell. Kennedy and others came too.

On July 29th we reached the scene of the murder which I estimated to be a distance from Cloncurry 200 miles, Carl Creek 80 miles, Kamilaroi 60 miles, Calton Hills 50 miles and situated on Mistake Creek, an eastern tributary of Gunpowder Creek which itself is a western tributary of the Leichardt River.

There we found Mr Powell's body which, owing to the cold weather, was in a good state of preservation and was identified without difficulty both by Mr Kennedy and myself.

We buried Powell's body. At the head of the grave, we marked a tree to show it was Powell's burial spot.

We started out after the blacks on the next day. Because the blacks had driven the horses and cattle with them it was very easy to follow their trail although the country traversed was mountainous and extremely rough.

We passed through ten camps, in all of which cattle had been killed and, in some cases, yards had been made to hold them.

After travelling 20 miles, we dropped into a deep gorge in Gunpowder Creek and there detected the smoke of a campfire curling upwards. An hour before sundown I had my troopers in ambush round the camp. It was a very large camp with upwards of 150 blacks in it.

Trooper Billy, acting on my orders, summoned them to surrender in their own language; but they resisted, and as further hesitation would have involved the escape of the offenders and possibly the destruction of my little party, I gave the order to fire and thirty of the blacks were shot.

Trooper Larry was knocked down by a black, but beyond that we had no further casualties.

Many blacks escaped but my detachment was not strong enough to admit of my doing more. In the camp we recovered seven horses, two riding saddles, one pack saddle, a shotgun, a revolver, cartridges, tobacco, blankets, clothing and all Mr Powell's camp equipment. They had killed all the cattle with the exception of five head which were too footsore to drive home with us so had to be left.

My detachment subsequently patrolled up the western branch of the Leichardt River across the divide and down the Wills to Teddington Lock. I had hoped that there I might meet the Burke River Detachment but I heard nothing of them.

Between the scene of the murder and the head of the Wills, we broke up and dispersed four large mobs of blacks, one of which, I was informed by the gins, had been watching Mulligan's prospecting camp on the Leichardt for some days with a view to making an attack upon it and as they were within a mile of that camp when I came upon them I think it probable that such was their intention. I cautioned Mr Mulligan to be very careful and I did not think that he would neglect any precautions.

We returned to Barracks on the 18th instead and reported myself on the 19th. The horses have suffered much through losing shoes in the mountains and doing long stages with insufficient grain and water and now require a spell. The trip was a most arduous one and hard tramping on foot amongst mountains on a short allowance of rations told considerably on myself and my troopers, but I think the blacks have had a caution which will exercise a deterrent effect upon them for some time to come.

Chapter 21

LIVING IN A WILDERNESS

ERNEST HENRY, 1885

'I don't know how you manage to move amongst the Kalkadoons the way you do but you've got to be more careful, Henry,' Urquhart told me. 'In fact it's much too dangerous, right now, to be prospecting the mountains.'

I was, of course, appreciative of his solicitude. But I was not about to tell him that I would continue riding into the hills to look for copper. Nor did I want to mention that the Kalkadoons were actually helping me locate new copper lodes.

But I was certainly interested in his description of what happened at Calton Downs. It was territory I pioneered, out on Gunpowder Creek and Alexander Kennedy and James Powell had taken up the run following my proposals to them.

And now Powell was dead.

It was early 1885 when we spoke about the killings and the conflict. We were sitting just outside my hut at the Great Australian mine at Cloncurry.

'Poor Kennedy, he must have taken it pretty hard,' I said. 'He'd been in partnership with Powell for a number of years.'

'They all took it hard on Calton Downs,' Urquhart replied. 'It's not just the dead that you grieve for. It's the family they leave behind, the people who knew and loved them. And I don't want that happening to you or the ones you would leave behind.'

I know that Urquhart spoke with my interests in mind, but I could not, honestly, say that I would not venture into the mountains again. There were still potentially rich copper areas to be found.

'Many people think that with the recent punitive action that the Kalkadoons are a beaten race,' said Urquhart. 'That may be the case but, in my opinion, one white man in their mountain region is still a person at risk.'

I have had time to think on what Urquhart said that day. About living in a wilderness populated by few white men and many blackfellows. And survival. How was it that some survived and others suffered horrific deaths? Was it blind fate? Or could one shape that fate?

Had I simply been lucky? Or had, what I had done, helped me live and survive in the wilderness?

I have always held a regard for the natives of this country. They are a primitive people but, I find, more childlike than malevolent.

I still recall the first I encountered. On my ride from Sydney to Moreton Bay in 1858, about Christmas time. There was a hut on the Namoi River at a crossing there.

There was only a blackfellow and his gin living at the hut. They were employed cutting down the burrs. He was certainly a most respectful black. He gave me a first-rate supper which consisted of fish he had just caught in the river and baked in the ashes. He was a lively fellow, chatting away the whole time.

He began, 'You know me not like other blackfellow, other blackfellow fool. Me half white fellow, live like white fellow. Any man come to my place me make him welkin.'

In many cases, the natives I saw in my travels were timid rather than aggressive. Often, they would run away from me, shouting and howling but fleeing, nevertheless. Sometimes they would scale up trees and mutter what I took to be oaths. On such occasions I would endeavour to make friendly sounds and take no action that would alarm these people.

I recall one occasion when we were on the Cape River. We had, earlier that day, feasted on a couple of black ducks I had shot. Just before making camp that day we came upon a blackfellow. He was up a tree cutting out an opossum with a stone tomahawk.

He did not see us nor did we him till we were close under the tree. At first, he seemed dumb with surprise and terror. At last, he recovered a bit and then let out on us a volley evidently entreating us to leave him and ending every oration with a loud yell to his gins who were camped up the river a bit.

From the state he was in, I don't think he could ever have seen a white man before.

We found his gins camped a little higher up the river. They had fled and left all their goods behind them.

We moved up the river about a mile and camped.

Then there was the occasion on the Suttor River where we found a blackfellow and his gin fishing in a waterhole. They dived when they saw us. It was a long time before we could see them. At last, our blackboy pointed out the man to us. He had come up among a few reeds the opposite side with just his face above water. He remained there without moving until one of our party went to the edge of the water to look at some fish the natives had caught.

The gin happened to be just opposite amongst the reeds although we had not perceived her. But when the blackfellow saw our man approach her so close, he jumped up and called to her. She followed his example and they both walked up the opposite bank jabbering and motioning to us to move on. Which we did, not wishing to frighten them.

Higher up the river we came upon a whole mob of natives scattered all over the bed of the river, fishing and hunting.

About a dozen gins took to one waterhole with their children who they carried on their backs. The gins kept diving down and coming up almost immediately, fearful of drowning their children.

We passed on so as not to frighten them.

I always went armed, of course. But only in extreme cases was I prepared to discharge such arms. One such occasion arose when we were exploring the area that was subsequently to become the Hughenden run. A gentleman named Devlin and I, together with a blackboy named Alex were involved.

We were camped on the Flinders, a river that empties into the Gulf of Carpentaria. Devlin and I walked to the top of a small range on the other side of which was a valley, the most beautiful spot I have seen in this country. The hills and ranges on either side were grassed and open almost to their summits, dotted here and there with pretty myall trees, the valley being a succession of downs also studded with clumps of myalls.

The next day we left Alex, the blackboy, in camp and rode over as much of the country as we could. Soon after we had left our camp, we met some gins who, becoming frightened, started shouting for their men.

We had left Alex a pistol, a double-barrelled gun and a carbine in case there was any trouble.

When we got back, Alex rode to meet us. He showed us eleven spears stuck in the creek bed where our camp was located. Our camp was on the dry riverbed behind some large gum trees, about 20 to 30 yards from one of the banks. The whole bed was about 120 yards across.

At noon, while we were away, Alex crossed to the other side of the river to get water. He heard the cooee of blacks down the river. On looking in that direction he saw the natives and ran and caught his horse and brought him to the camp area. He tried to saddle the horse but, before he could, some twenty men armed with spears and shields appeared on the bank immediately opposite the camp and began throwing spears at him. The gum trees gave him some protection from the attack.

Alex fired the pistol and then the gun. Although he hit no one, the firing at first drove the natives back. He then retreated a little distance to another tree against which the carbine was resting. The carbine was his last chance. The blacks were now advancing with their *nulla-nullas*.

Alex took a steady aim and put a bullet through the shield of the foremost native. The rest of the natives fled.

Much to Alex's disgust, the man he had knocked over got up and followed, though at a much slower pace.

Alex then loaded the gun with powder only and, mounted, galloped after them, yelling and firing until the natives disappeared amongst some rocks down the river.

Not everyone holds the same sentiments as I do. Kennedy, heaven help him, would not trust a native within spear-throwing distance.

I recall being out bush with him one day. Suddenly Kennedy's horse rears and, at the same time, a spear goes shooting past him. Well, Kennedy takes off after the native but the blackfellow, discarding everything he carried, took to the rocky ground and Kennedy had to abandon the chase – but not before firing several shots at the fleeing man.

I told him at that time that it wasn't right to go shooting at Aboriginals like that.

To which he replied, 'Well, if I hadn't had a go at him, he would have got one of us with the next spear.'

There were, in some cases, those who tried to care for the natives, to reduce the conflict between whites and blacks. Like the Christison brothers. They came to an arrangement with their natives to let them hunt and live tribally on the Christison run as long as the natives did not interfere with the stock in any way. That seemed to work out.

And there was Neil MacDonald, the pioneer settler of Glenroy who took in 'Tubbie Terrier', who has survived Battle Mountain. Not only that, but MacDonald protected the native warrior from the Native Mounted Police who hunted down Aboriginals following the fight.

I guess I can only speak for myself. In my own dealings with these primitive people, I tried to be friendly wherever possible, to respect them and their customs and not to abuse them. I found that they generally reacted very well to such an approach. There was just the one occasion when things did not turn out well.

Chapter 22

IN PURSUIT

FREDERIC URQUHART
QUEENSLAND COMMISSIONER OF POLICE
1919

There are some instances, within a lifetime packed with unforgettable events, that remain with you throughout the rest of your life. The battle of the mountain is something I will not forget.

As Commissioner of Police, of course, I now have direct access to the records of those days and, occasionally, I re-read some of those reports I wrote so long ago. In doing so, I relive those days.

It was in summer, 1885, February in fact. And Cloncurry was in its full heat as we set off to investigate the incident that had occurred at Granada Station. Even for a young man, I was just thirty years old, the heat was still something to contend with.

I had received an urgent message from that run and so moved my men quickly to that location. At Granada I found the details of the complaint. The station hands had been absent from the homestead at the time. This gave the blacks the opportunity to come up and drive the Chinese cook away. They then helped themselves to rations.

Their tracks were evident, and we followed them up for three or four days. Their path was even easier to follow, as, on their way, the natives had recently killed cattle.

It was a Kalkadoon blackboy I had with me at the time who informed me that the mob we were following included the blacks who had killed William Woods on the Dugald in November '84. In addition, the same blacks had killed another man at Cabbage Tree Creek, in January '85.

When we caught up with the natives, they drew off to one side. That, as any bushman will tell you, is a sure sign of mischief.

I got my Kalkadoon blackboy to talk to the mob and explain to them that, if they would give up the murderers to me, I would not molest the others.

The blacks refused the offer outright. They assailed us with a barrage of yells and showers of sticks, stones and spears. Luckily, we dodged these missiles as the savages fled in all directions.

My troopers opened fire and down went a number of the natives. Those who were shot included five who were actually concerned with the two murders. Among those felled was an infamous savage known as 'Mickey'.

'Mickey' was known throughout the region as a black involved in every local depredation. A nasty villain. He was connected with all outrages that had happened to stations along the Leichardt River.

Following the affray, we detained thirty-five gins. They were later to give me further details of one of the murders which involved 'Mickey' and, in fact, take me to the place where this outrage had occurred.

They were to take me to Cabbage Tree Creek to point out where 'Mickey' and other blacks had killed an unnamed white man. The man, they said, had been riding up a creek and got off his horse to have a drink. A native drove a spear through him and 'Mickey' finished him with a tomahawk, the gins said. I could not find his body, but from what I later found in a black's camp, I estimate this man died on or about 2 January 1885. Unfortunately, the man's identity remains a mystery. There are, however, numbers of men about in the ranges that nobody knows anything of and no notice is taken of their goings and comings.

Detailed information on the second murder involving 'Mickey' was later provided by an Aboriginal named Billy who knew where this second man was killed. This was a patch of turpentine scrub running into the Dugald River five miles north of Granada. The man had met blacks there and took a gin from them and while he was camping with her under a tree was killed by the blacks.

If this is true, and I believe it was, the man brought his death upon himself.

This was all revealed to me after the expedition I am now relating.

But, during the night after our first encounter with the native mob, we saw a fire. It was blazing on the top of a nearby mountain. The gins informed us that there was another large mob of Aboriginals camped on the mountain.

So, an hour before daylight we set out for the mountain. As we arrived at the base of the mountain, we got an idea of its size. The mountain stood some 800 feet high, and it was steep. So steep, in fact, that we were forced to leave the horses in a gully at the bottom. The only way we could ascend was on foot and we began this advance just as day was breaking.

The party moved up silently over the rock-studded hillside where anthills protruded like giant teeth. We had every prospect of taking the mountain-top mob by complete surprise. But we had not bargained on the 'lookout'.

We were about halfway up the mountain when we heard the alarm. It came from a gin who was among the rocks above us.

We could have been walking into a carefully planned ambush, the way it happened then. But I think it was just that the Kalkadoons were what everyone thought them to be – true warriors. The result of the alarm ringing out through the dawn air was immediate. The blacks were in readiness for just such an attack and we looked up to see a perfect avalanche of rocks and stones being rolled and thrown down on us.

All of this was accompanied by savage battle cries from those hurling these weapons. As I dodged out of the way, I managed to look up and was surprised, somewhat, about the size of the mob above us. It was hard to get a good measure of their strength. The only way to calculate that was through the sighting of heads popping up above rocks or upraised arms ready to direct spears our way. But even from those glimpses, it was obvious that the natives above us were there in considerable numbers. Because they were so well hidden behind the rocks, we could not get any good use of our firearms.

In fact, the natives were situated above rocks above us which seemed to form a natural parapet. That fortification along the top of the mountain was another obstacle we would have to overcome.

I called on my men to push on up the hill and here there was an episode of real shame. Some of my troopers, three in fact, displayed the most disgusting cowardice. They refused to advance while the stone throwing continued.

However, two other troopers, Billy No. 1 and Billy No. 2, continued the ascent and we were at that point where we began to approach the top and the stones ceased coming. The last 50 yards, however, was a precipice, very hard to climb.

I have little doubt that if the blacks had stuck to their course, if they had continued their assault as they earlier had done, they would have done for us right there. But they didn't.

When we got to the top, we found the blacks had bolted. They had gone. Across the mountain.

It was at this time that I noticed I'd been injured. In the heat of the action, I really had not had time to think about it, but I now saw I had a nasty bruise on one leg. A lump of rock had broken at my feet and fragments had dashed my leg. Trooper Billy No. 1 was wounded with contusions on the shoulder where he had been hit by a rock.

With the blacks having fled, we headed down the mountain as soon as we got our breath. We got our horses and rode around the mountain and picked up the tracks of the fleeing savages. But they took off into very rough country where horses could not travel so we had to give up the chase.

I don't remember this occasion for any real success of the venture but for the challenges it posed to our band.

I refer back to the report I sent, in those earlier times, to my Sub-Inspector in Muttaburra and which, subsequently, was forwarded to the then Commissioner.

And I still agree with my opinion of those days –'The blacks in this district are bad and neither conciliation or retribution seems to have any effect.'

Chapter 23

METICULOUS PLANNING

Arthur Henry

1900

Some people say my brother, Ernest, was rash. But to me he was someone who was always planning ahead.

An adventurer, yes! But then our family comes from a long line of such people; and there is always a matter of chance in being so.

Our family, if you dig far enough back in time, were Scots. We came from Stirlingshire, but our family migrated to Jamaica where we were involved in the sugar industry. Our grandfather, James Henry, was a sugar plantation owner. James, in fact, was appointed a Member of the Jamaican Legislative Assembly.

When our grandfather died, his wife, Susannah, took their sons, James (our father) and Charles Edward, back to England.

Our father married Mary Francis Norris, the fourth daughter of John Norris of Hughenden Manor, Buckinghamshire. They had four sons – James, Ernest, myself and Alfred – born in that order. Ernest was a little over a year older than me. There were some six years between myself and Alfred. The three younger sons came to settle in Australia. Our oldest brother, James, took up tea planting in India.

Brother Ernest was little more than a lad, about sixteen, when he first left home as a junior officer on the SS *Victoria* of the Australian Royal Mail Service Company. In this way he visited Adelaide, Melbourne and Sydney in 1853. But his career there was short-lived for, on his return voyage, war had been declared on Russia.

Ernest's father bought him a commission in the army. He gained that when he passed the examination at the Royal Military College of Sandhurst. Ernest was gazetted an Ensign in the 72nd Highlanders, the regiment in which our father had served as a captain twenty years before.

Shortly after that he went with the regiment to the Crimea where two things happened – the war ended, and he was invalided home. By now he was barely nineteen and barracks life back in Britain did little for his restless spirit.

In 1857, Ernest left home once more, this time for Australia.

His adventures, and some of the sketches he made and sent to us, filled my youthful years. For Ernest, above all else, was a letter writer. And even allowing for the erratic mail services of those times, our family received many a tale of life in the colonies.

Part of his grand plan, I know, was to build his own pastoral empire and his brothers, myself and Alfred, were always a part of that plan.

I left home to join Ernest at the end of 1861. In the comparatively short time he had been here, Ernest had done – to me – so many wondrous things.

He had, initially, walked all the way from Melbourne, where he landed, to Sydney.

Then he rode from Brisbane to Moreton Bay where he met up with a gentleman named George Elphinstone Dalrymple. In doing so, he became a member of Dalrymple's party that explored the region of Bowen and the Burdekin River. Somewhere in the midst of all this activity, Ernest had taken the time to gain valuable pastoral experience on a number of properties.

By the time I arrived to join him, he held a station – Baroondah – on the Dawson River and was busy establishing what he always claimed was the jewel among his properties –Mt McConnell on the Burdekin.

He had before him enough work to fill the time of four men. But he was always thinking of and planning for his family.

When he knew I was coming, together with Alfred, to join him, he wrote to me from Baroondah in June 1861.

He expressed his delight at our imminent arrival in the Colony of Queensland.

'I trust you will like the life out here as well as I do,' he wrote.

I had asked him to send a list of what I should bring out.

He recommended I bring with me only what was necessary 'as you will find much luggage greatly in your way.'

'There are some things in the way of dress, however, which you might as well get at home as you will there get them better made and much cheaper.'

'For instance,' he continued, 'I should recommend your having two or three pairs of <u>strong</u> shooting boots and be sure they are made plenty large enough as tight boots in this country cause one great pain when riding in the sun. Also, one pair of <u>strong</u> top boots; if you get tops to them, have them made of black glazed leather; two pairs of <u>strong</u>

Bedford card trousers, or one pair trousers and one of pantaloons. Crimean shirts above all things, you will find them very serviceable on-board ship as they are easily washed, which the sailors will do for you and in the bush nothing else is worn; also a few white duck trousers; with more than that, do not lumber yourselves, excepting of course what you have by you and what is necessary for the voyage.'

He advised us to get a large hold for all, for our brushes, combs, sponges etc. and hang it at length in our cabin.

'You will find it immensely useful, also a large bag for your dirty clothes.'

'If you can procure them, bring out a stag hound or a blood hound or even a couple of large fox hounds. We want in this country heavier dogs than what we call kangaroo dogs. Either of the above-mentioned dogs would make a good cross.'

On our arrival in Sydney, Ernest recommended we stay at the Royal Hotel.

'It is like all Colonial inns – very expensive. But as there is a weekly boat to Brisbane, the chances are you will only be obliged to remain a few days there.'

Ernest then listed the various sites that should be seen during a brief stay in Sydney.

'If you require a horse for hire, go to Buchan Thompson's stables,' he advised.

He also promised to advise some of his friends in Sydney of the date of our arrival so that 'they will show you the place.'

That was my big brother, Henry. Some may say he was rash. But none could deny he was a meticulous planner.

Chapter 24

UP IN THE AIR

ALEXANDER KENNEDY

1926

Of all the adventures I have had in my life, flying must surely be the most enjoyable.

I thought, when I was a young man and I came with cattle and sheep to this vast empty land that I would never, ever, enjoy such freedom. I was mistaken. There is nothing quite like being up there, with the clouds, with the birds and looking down on a land I'm not fighting but filled with wonderment about its mountains and plains and rivers.

To think, I can cross journeys in an hour when once it took weeks of struggle and sweat and not just a few harsh words to horse or bullock.

My one regret, I suppose, is I can't share the experience with many of my old friends. People like Powell, Henry and Sheaffe. But, I dare say, they're using wings of a different sort in another world. Well, at least I hope they are.

I know we'd have had a good old laugh up here in the air. Henry would, I'm sure, be constantly on the lookout for copper outcrops.

'Look, Kennedy,' he'd be saying, 'can you see that outcrop down there. I'll bet there's a lode to be found, right there.'

And Sheaffe, too, would be looking closely at the watercourses, at the grasses, and calculating how he could make a claim on any good land not yet inhabited.

And we'd all – every one of us – be looking down and pointing out places we'd inched through in the early days. Places where we'd run out of food. Areas where we we'd gone without water for more than a day and kept going just on a hope and a prayer. We would have remembered the plains which so often were either parched with drought or bogged by floodwaters. If only they were here now. I love flying but it would be so much better to share it with old friends.

I know Christina would have loved having aeroplanes flying into and out of the west. When she first came out here as my wife, she was often the only woman within 300 miles. That was a great burden for her. Just getting supplies from down south often took up to six months. Not much chance of getting essentials in a hurry, let alone keeping up with fashion.

But flying over this country is, every time, like opening a book, re-reading the events that happened down there in the plains and the mountains.

Like Duchess. My son, Jack, discovered the copper lode there back in 1897. That was a good find. Ten years later the mine sold for £15,000. Of course, since then, it has gone on to produce some £2 million worth of copper.

I look at the plains that spread endlessly south from here and I recall the droving teams that took our cattle to markets in Adelaide and Wodonga in Victoria.

Some years were great. 1879 – we overlanded 300 bullocks to Adelaide, and they fetched £11 a head. Then you had 1880 when we sent 1 000 head to Wodonga. By the time we had paid the £1 border tax on each beast, they brought just £3 each. Thank God, at least that border tax no longer applies since federation.

I tell you, these aeroplanes are a marvellous thing. They're going to make a big difference to those of us in the bush. But why the damned hell couldn't they have been invented sixty years ago?

Some people thought I was too old to go flying when I turned eighty-seven. But I soon disabused them of such notions.

I fell in love with the idea long before I got off the ground. I guess it started with the fighter planes flying in the Great War. And then, when the pilots and their planes came home, and we could see them up close.

One of those occasions was in November 1919. This was the first time an aircraft made a crossing of the continent, south to north. The aircraft, a BE2E which started out from Melbourne, was fitted with extra fuel tanks. Spare parts were packed into the fuselage.

By the time the aircraft reached Cloncurry it was experiencing some difficulties. In fact, by that stage of its journey, major engine repairs were required. They replaced a cylinder with a spare they were carrying. But they also needed to replace four exhaust valves.

It was the local railway men who came to the rescue. They used a lathe at their workshop to fashion the valves from an old car axle.

It was in 1920, actually, that I got into the air for the first time. A joyride over Brisbane, to be precise.

The returned heroic flyers were being increasingly seen out over the western plains. Mainly raising money for peace loans. You could go aloft for between three and five guineas a ride. I so much enjoyed talking with these former servicemen about their flying experiences and their journeys through our own country.

Of course, there were the doubting Thomases. And there were those who, no matter what you said, would never put any significant space between themselves and the ground.

I'd chide them. I'd tell them they were safer in an aeroplane than they were in their own bed.

And, right from the start, I knew how much the aeroplane could benefit the outback.

Undoubtedly, Kingsford Smith's England-to-Australia flight had a big impact on local thinking. Particularly as the plane landed in Cloncurry. Such flights showed the public how reliable aviation was.

Fergus McMaster arrived in Cloncurry one day looking for local backing for a new air company he was calling the Queensland and Northern Territory Aerial Services. I was on his list of prospective supporters.

He told me, in some detail, about the plan for the company. First of all, the whole of western Queensland was to be exploited for joyriding and air taxi possibilities; then, if experience showed that a reasonable amount of success could be anticipated, all the western railheads from Charleville to Cloncurry were to be linked up by air, with ultimate extensions to Brisbane and Sydney and across the Barkley Tableland to Daly Waters and Darwin – an ambitious scheme indeed for those days and one requiring firm visions in the face of adverse criticism.

When he had finished, he asked me directly not if I'd back the company but how much I'd contribute.

I told him £200. He asked me for £250.

I agreed. But I had one condition – that I would be the company's first passenger when regular flights began.

'Oh, no!' said McMaster. 'We couldn't consider that. You are too old a man.'

'Never mind, those are my conditions,' I told him.

And I got my way.

Chapter 25

DIFFERENT PATHS

ALEXANDER KENNEDY

1926

We came, almost, from opposite ends of the social scale, Henry and I.

Henry was a man of substance, even before he arrived here, family connections, land and some wealth. A man with a history, even before he embarked from the homeland.

Not so, me.

I'm given to understand, from Henry himself, that he's Scottish, removed somewhat by a few generations and a couple of countries in which his forebears lived. So, maybe, deep down in our history, that's part of the reason we were friends for so long.

But while Henry's people were very much a part of the English gentry, it wasn't until later life that my mother and father even learned to speak English. Their native language was Gaelic.

Henry's early life, so he told me, was one of public schooling and then into his cadetship in the commercial navy.

We came, originally, from Dunkfield, Perthshire. We had a hard life in that country. And later, when we went to Forfarshire where my father became a forester on a local estate, I went out to work in the fields. That was after I turned fifteen and finished my schooling at a Presbyterian Church school.

Ten hours a day. Much of it in sub-zero temperatures. And for what – a pittance by comparison with what men make here in Australia. And all on the regular diet of the 'brose cap' – our bowls filled with oatmeal and milk and water. Aye, it doesn't bear comparison with a good beef dinner and vegetables I now enjoy. I doubt that Henry often tasted oatmeal.

In many ways it was easier for Henry to make his way in this new land. He arrived, here, for instance, with a saddlebag-full of letters of introduction. And those were introductions to people of substance in this country.

There was, for example, the MacLeays to whom Henry had a letter of introduction. Using this, he arranged to get to a station on the Murrumbidgee where he was able to learn the sheep business.

That, together with family acquaintances who had already migrated from the home country, helped smooth his pathway once he got here.

Not so, me.

There was no one waiting to meet or greet me when the 'Eagle' landed me in Rockhampton in 1861. Every step of the way, I had to make my *own* way. Can you imagine coming from the freezing fields of Scotland to the sunburnt bush of Queensland? 'Twas a mighty adjustment to be made. And then there was the burden of being an unknown 'new chum'.

It was hard work, and it went on for years until I built up both a reputation and enough money to start off on my own.

That, too, was something that Henry had to do – to become a part of his new country, to come to terms with it, with the land and its challenges.

And, I would say, Henry did this with audacity. When he left the Murrumbidgee in late 1858, at the end of the shearing there, he went back to Melbourne to start on what is, in any country, an epic trek. By himself, on horse, he cut close to 1500 miles through the bush to the Macintyre River.

He told me that, at times, it felt rather lonely. But, he admitted, 'I had my books to keep me company.' A great reader was Henry.

But, by comparison, Henry had managed to accumulate some three properties within three or four years of arriving in Melbourne. He had the background – the contacts and the family money – that helped him in those early years.

Some people may think I am saying I'm a self-made man whereas Henry had an easier time of it. 'Tis true, to some extent.

But that's not the point I am making here.

It's that, in this bold new colony, there were great opportunities not just for those with money but also those without a lot of it. I just happened to be in the second mob. And, so, too, did Henry become when the bottom of the market fell through in the mid-1860s.

For many it was their end. They crawled away from the fight. But for Henry, it was just the start of a new struggle. And he, like I had earlier done, was starting from scratch. In fact, he was at a greater disadvantage than the ones I had faced on arrival.

For Henry, being from the class he was, had to face down the ignominy of failure. And that was harder to do with his background than with my own. More was expected of him from his own.

I, on the other hand, had only my own expectations to meet in my drive to succeed in this brutal and bountiful land. I had no debt of honour by reason of birth.

Chapter 26

FAIR EXCHANGE

Arthur Henry, 1900

Remember how I said that Ernest was a great planner? It seemed that even the smallest details were important to him. That was made clear to me and our other brother, Alfred, while we were busy helping to establish Mt McConnell.

Some things, of course, no one can foresee. And this happened when Ernest was making his application for this Burdekin River run. He took his applications for the property and set out for Sydney to obtain a licence to occupy.

But after the long journey to Sydney, he found himself defeated by recent developments in the colony. Just five days before he reached Sydney, Queensland's first Governor-designate, Sir George Bowen, had left for Brisbane bearing the charter of Queensland's independence.

In fact, it was not until 1862 that the leasehold of this land was officially granted. That was of no small concern to my brother.

But this was something outside Ernest's control. What he did do, however, was to pay close attention to whatever he could.

The incident I refer to involved the Aboriginals on Mt McConnell station. There weren't a lot of blacks on the run. And those who were there were not as treacherous as those in other parts of the north.

In fact, Ernest had little trouble with the natives. If anything, he would try to win the blacks to his side.

We, Alfred and I, had been out timber-splitting and, after a long day on the job, we'd forgotten to bring the iron wedges back with us to the homestead. Henry was not happy with what had happened when we told him.

'You've got to realise,' he said to us, 'that out here we're far away from the nearest supply post. It could take months, in fact, for us to get replacements.'

Alfred and I were most contrite.

'Well,' Ernest said, 'we've got to ride out first thing tomorrow and retrieve them.'

So, we were all up and mounted at daybreak. We rode to the area and when we could not find the wedges where we thought we'd left them, we split up and moved out in separate directions.

It was Ernest who got the trail first.

He told us afterwards that he heard blacks in a bushy area.

'They were laughing and talking and were busily chopping out possums from some trees.'

'I saw, at once, that they were using our wedges,' said Ernest. 'They had used the wedges as axes by fixing them into handles, much the same way as they make their own stone axes.'

'I must say that I was most impressed by their ingenuity,' he commented.

He was so impressed that he rode up to the Aboriginals and, after ensuring them he meant them no harm, he offered to swap the wedges for some of our own steel tomahawks – we had more of them than we had wedges – if the Aboriginals would bring the wedges back to the homestead.

This they subsequently did, and the exchange was made with no ill feeling on either side.

Chapter 27

TRUST

ERNEST HENRY'S BLACKBOY, DICK, 1870

They have no stories except of themselves. These white fellows.

They are in the land but not a part of it.

No stories about the serpents and spirits that shaped it.

They say they *own* the land. And I have, indeed, seen the pieces of paper with the writings that say the land from that river all the way to the far away mountains belongs to them. And that they can bring their sheep and their cattle and fill up the land and drink all the water and shoot other animals like kangaroos and birds in the sky. And use all the water, whatever may be available, for their own animals.

And their pieces of paper, so I reckon, also tells them they have the right to keep other people off the land they *own* – even if those people have called that land their home for untold years before the white fellow came.

You see, here's what I can't understand. It's their land because someone far away says this is so. And that we, the people who have lived here since the dreamtime, have no right to be here if the white man says we don't.

So, we have been swept away. Homeless. No kin, no culture, no country.

And those who do not know this land try to live in, and against it. And against us.

Oh, they will use us. When it suits them. And I have been with my boss, Mr Henry, since I was a youth. I am now starting to become an old man. And I wonder, now, what will become of me as I do grow older. I know that many other 'boys' are just tossed away by their bosses when they are too old to become useful any longer. I hope that will not happen to me.

Though we have worked together, eaten together, ridden together, he is still 'Boss' and I am still his 'boy'. I will continue to be a 'boy' in the white man's eyes until I die.

I have been with Mr Henry since the days on the Dawson River where my tribe once lived. It was when he was stocking his property 'Baroondah' and, as a young man I helped muster the stock there. I was – still am—a good horseman. And he liked what I could do and took me with him when he was taking stock to a new northern country, he called the Burdekin.

There was not much left for me to stay in my own country. Our way of life had gone – or, more so, the life my tribe had known. And I enjoyed the life on horseback. So, I agreed.

Since then, it has been some twenty years. Most of it has been for food, clothing, and a roof over my head. Some money – but just a few coins that rattle in my pockets. That was a really big reason that the settlers had their blackboys – it cost them very little to do so. If they'd had whites working for them, it would have cost them a whole lot more.

Sometimes when he was mad with me, he'd say, 'Dick, you're not worth two plugs of tobacco.'

One day when we were on the track, after we'd been together for many years, I asked him, 'Boss, why do you say I'm not worth two plugs of tobacco?'

'Because that's what I paid for you when I bought you at the station down on the Dawson,' he said.

One day, when we were together with another 'boy' and his boss, I heard that man tell his 'boy' he wasn't worth a plug of tobacco.

And I knew what he meant.

So, I told the other 'boy', a man called Tom, 'You know, I'm not worth twice what you're not worth.'

Being cheap labour was part of the reason the whites took us with them ... We also knew the country better than the whites. How to survive long periods in hard areas. The whites, it seemed, learned from early mistakes made by their early explorers who went off into the bush and died there.

'Boys' like me knew where to look out for water in dry spells. We knew how to follow animal tracks to water holes. We knew what to look for in bush tucker.

And they figured it best to have a blackboy beside them when they went into Aboriginal country. They hoped that we would be able to help them with any natives they met along the way. And also, that we might be able to warn them, the white explorers, about any possible attacks by local blackfellows. They figured we would know when approaching blackfellows were likely to be friendly or when they were likely to attack.

There were always the everyday things. Up early each day to get the campfire going, get the horses ready for the day. Mustering the sheep or the cattle, rounding them up and bringing them back to camp of a night.

So, a blackboy had plenty to do. But there was also plenty of adventure.

If someone asked me, I'd say we've never been friends. 'Boss' and 'boy', after all these years. But a little more, I think. For we have shared a lot and much of it a hard lot during our time in the bush. We've grown to rely on each other, us two travellers.

And we do trust each other.

I knew if we were off for whoever knows where – and that's somewhere where no white man has trekked before – that the 'Boss' would find his way there. And, what used to amaze me in the first year or so of our travels, Henry could usually tell me how long it would take before we reached a particular spot.

He had this round thing with a floating arrow in it, something he called a 'compass' which he was using as we made our way along. He told me it was something which sailors used to find their way home when they were at sea. I was just glad that it worked in the middle of the bush as well. But, just occasionally, I think even Henry was worried when we were deep in the country.

And he's a tough man. You would not think it, to look at him. He's as tall as some of those big anthills you get in the bush. But he looked more like a sapling than a tree.

Apart from that time up in the Gulf, when the fever broke out there and Henry helped get the people over to Sweers Island, I've never seen him sick at all. Still, he was lucky then, too – lucky I was there to help him. I got him into shady cover and laid him down. He was in pain, a lot of it. And he was covered in sweat. The fever was eating him up. I stayed with him, rubbed him down with some terrible smelling medicine that came in a bottle. Don't know if that did any good at all. I was wiping him down with wet rags all the time and giving him water when I could get him to drink. I thought he would die. But he didn't.

Saw a horse fall on him once. That slowed him down, but only for a day or so.

Swimming – you should see him in the water. Like he's half fish. Now I can swim but I'm not going to do the things he does. In our travels we've come across many a swollen stream, sometimes flooded rivers. If there's been no other course, I've seen him jump in and swim those waters. And, on more than one occasion he's saved some poor fool who's been in trouble.

That reminds me of the day we were busy trying to get some heavy equipment through a river in flood. We were doing this at a point where you could still get over, but you would be up to your chest at points. Anyway, there's this big bloke, an Englishman, I think, and he tells Henry he wants to help.

Henry asks the man if he can swim.

'Course I can,' says the man.

'Can you handle this heavy stuff out there in the water?'

The big man laughed at Henry's question.

I could see the Boss wasn't sure about this, but he let the man go out carrying some big iron pieces. About halfway, when the water is over his waist, the big bloke stumbles and down goes the pieces.

Well, Henry was not too happy when the man drags himself back to the bank. But no amount of talk by Henry can get the man back into the river to save the equipment.

I guess I knew what was going to happen before the big bloke even went in. He was big, alright, but you could tell he thought he was even bigger. And, despite myself, I was wearing a silly grin all the time he was in the water. Henry, I guess, knew what I was thinking.

So, having failed to get the drenched man back into the water, he turned to me and said, 'Dick, you go get it.'

I found the pieces, stuck deep in the riverbed mud. And then I got back, got a rope and went back to tie the pieces to it, and we dragged them back to the shore.

I found it interesting that, although Henry had doubts from the start that his fellow countryman could do the job, he knew I could.

We trusted each other.

Chapter 28

THE NATIVE POLICE

QUEENSLAND POLICE COMMISSIONER URQUHART

1919

There was a time when people welcomed the Native Mounted Police in their area, when they demanded their presence. But, as the danger to the local people subsided, as they themselves were less at risk, it seemed the population of those centres were increasingly prone to criticise and demean the work that the Native Police had undertaken.

The acceptance of the Native Mounted Police was proportional to the local threat by the blacks.

To me, people seemed too quick to forget the frontier and how towns, and even cities, had been allowed to grow only after the danger of attacks from Aboriginals had been removed. And that the growth and prosperity these same people now enjoyed had relied upon the foundation that the Native Mounted Police had built.

I joined the Native Mounted Police as a young man. I didn't join up immediately on arriving here. It wasn't my first job. In fact, I had been a midshipman on a fully-rigged sailing ship, in the merchant marine, when I arrived in Queensland in 1857. I worked, variously, on a sugar plantation and then on a cattle station. When I turned twenty, I joined the Electric Telegraph Department and worked in the far north of the state. It was here that I first had contact with the Native Police who were patrolling that area as we worked our way through the bush and jungle in the Normanton region. Up there I was doing repair work in an area where not only was the climate extreme, but we also had the everyday threat of sudden attack by the aborigines. I learned firsthand not only bushmanship but also a lot about the fear that people on the frontier faced in those days.

I had the opportunity, also, to talk with the officers of the Native Mounted Police and what they had to say undoubtedly bent me towards their ranks. What they told me, and from what I could see of their activities, showed me that these officers really enjoyed their freedom from restraint, the independent open-air life that they enjoyed, though within a disciplined force. There was also more than a hint of danger about the job.

Sometimes when they visited our camp I would sit with the officer, a sub-inspector they were called. They could see I was interested and gave me insights into the ways of the force.

'Your troopers are the key to much of what good you do out here,' one of them told me as we sat around the campfire one evening. 'Good troopers make the difference. They can track an ant over stone-hard ground. They'll find marauding blacks in the most impossible places.'

'And they'll look after you,' he continued. 'You'll rely on them for hunting for food, for finding water where you would swear there's none.'

'In my own case,' he told me, 'I was once down with dreadful fever. I had no other white man within hundreds of miles. One of the gins, a trooper's wife, took care of me. Building a fire to keep me warm, changing my bedding, making me tea and cold drinks, whatever worked. I would not be here today without her ministering. She was a black angel.'

The secret, he informed me was to be firm with the troopers, never surrendering authority over them but always to treat them with respect.

It was in 1882 that I had to make my decision. At that time, the Telegraph service told me I would receive an automatic promotion to a clerical position within the Department. I did not fancy being behind a desk. I enjoyed, relished, the outdoor bush life. Also, I realised that, beyond the immediate promotion, there was little prospect for my further advancement within the Department in the short term. Promotion would be slow and difficult to obtain.

I had been considering the Native Police as a career and had written to my godfather, General Fielding, because of his contacts within the Queensland government.

I remember writing to the General, so that he could forward to others my background experience and aptitudes. Almost all of this he, of course, already knew, but my letter to him was in the form, in reality, of an application to join the Native Police. As part of that letter, I stated:

As regards character and education, I believe I am fitted for the post I wish to obtain. My father was a major in the Royal Artillery, and I was partially educated with my brother, now a Lieutenant in the same corps with a view to my following in the same profession. I can confidently refer to my career in the Telegraph Department as a guarantee of sobriety good character etc.

I think also I possess some special qualifications. Both before and since I joined the Telegraph, I have mixed much with the blacks both in company with Native Police and at other times and I have a practical knowledge of the languages spoken by several of the tribes of this district.

I showed, also that I was aware of Government policy of the day stating knowledge of the conciliatory policy adopted by the present Government towards the blacks.

I explained, in my letter to General Fielding:

My very best endeavours will be used to carry that policy out. At the same time, I am fully aware that in cases of outrage committed by the blacks they must be dealt with promptly and firmly.

I received a telegraphic reply a little later from the General who was shortly heading for England. It said:

ELECTRIC TELEGRAPH, QUEENSLAND
FROM: 17 JANUARY 1882, BRISBANE
MESSAGE FOR: F.C. URQUHART ESQ.

Promise of first vacancy for you leave for England Friday.

General Fielding

Subsequent to that I joined the Native Mounted Police in May 1882 as a Cadet Sub-Inspector.

By the time I joined the force, it had already been the subject of a number of parliamentary enquiries. There had been attempts to shut down the Native Mounted Police because of what its critics called its 'excesses'. Others wanted to retain it, but in a modified form. In the end, the force remained because there was a need for it on the frontier. But it was recognised that officers needed to be better trained and that the force had to be more 'efficient'.

When I became part of this force, I entered as a Cadet Sub-Inspector, and I trained on the job with a superior officer before being posted to an area of my own responsibility. The structure of a policing unit, at that time, was typically one white officer with some six, maybe eight, native troopers attached to him. It was the white officer's responsibility to ensure that discipline and readiness of his troopers. The troopers used their innate skills of tracking and bushcraft to undertake the policing aspects of the unit.

Typically, the Sub-Inspector, in charge of the unit, would be housed in a cabin made from logs. The troopers would live within "gunyas" or tents.

The tribal nature of the black population was recognised in setting up the Native Police. Fealty and responsibility among the blacks is primarily to the tribe to which one belongs.

Those who established the Native Mounted Police recognised this and ensured, as much as possible, that native troopers were recruited from well outside the area they would patrol. Often they were recruited from different tribal groups to guard against any tribal banding within the one particular unit.

The troopers that I had with me in Cloncurry could have come from the Burnett region, an area which had already been subdued. I do not recall exactly, but I think this was so.

The troopers themselves enjoyed good money – one politician remarking at one time that they were paid more than British soldiers of that period. But they were equally drawn to the force by their love of horses, the uniforms they wore and the guns they were given.

When it came to a stand-up fight between troopers and local natives, there was little kinship consideration among the combatants. Both the natives and the troopers knew that it was a matter of kill or be killed.

Chapter 29

BEATING THE FLOODED BOWEN

Philip Frederic Sellheim

Queensland Under-Secretary for Mines

Brisbane, 1898

It is a great relief, believe me, to have now completed the new Mining Act. So much to embrace in this one piece of legislation but now it's done. I am hopeful that it will be of much use to our essential industry. Mining is already important to Queensland. I have no doubt that it will prove even more so in the years to come.

Last year's royal commission into the industry spelled out many of the areas that had to be addressed – reforming safety conditions within the industry, improving mining tenures and safeguards for both the big investor and the miner.

I am glad it's done. I'm not a young man anymore and I tire more easily now.

I remember when it was not so. When we were young and, it seemed, we could conquer all. And, I must admit that, in the framing of this legislation, my mind has sometimes wandered back to those days.

Is it not strange how fate twists and turns our lives so much that we find it hard to believe we are where we are, given how we started out?

It was like that with me and one of those many memorable people I have been remembering of late – Ernest Henry.

We began our acquaintance back in the late 1850s when we both signed up for Dalrymple's exploration of the Burdekin River. We were both looking for land we could open up.

Our backgrounds were different. Henry had migrated from England, from a well-established military background and had been engaged in the Crimean war although, as he related to me later, only fleetingly. He had actually come to Australia when he had signed onto a commercial shipping line.

Germany was my country of origin and, to tell the truth, my entry into the Australian pastoral business was much more likely than that of Henry. My family's association with the land went back to the tenth century when they settled in Hesse. My early studies had been at the Polytechnic Academy in Darmstadt. From there I went on to study sheep-breeding at the Royal Veterinary Academy of Berlin and the Agricultural Academy of Proskau in Upper Silesia.

Henry learned quickly from experience he gained on arrival in Australia in a number of stations down south. Like me, he was ambitious to get on in a country that favoured the bold.

But, just as Henry, initially, knew little about local industry and conditions, I knew little about swimming and it was because of this, as much as anything else he did – and that has been considerable – that I will long remember him among so many memorable people I've met since arriving in Australia back in 1855.

The event happened late 1861, or maybe early '62. The memory is somewhat hazy these days. But I remember it was when Henry was setting up his Mt McConnell run on the Burdekin. It wasn't long after he had moved a herd up from his property in the Burnett to Mt McConnell. That was a journey of some 600 miles and across country that was unoccupied except by the blacks. His brother, Arthur, had come out from England to join him on the Burdekin. I think it was the next year that they were joined by the youngest brother, Alfred.

In any case, I was managing Strathmore station on the Bowen River at the time and both Henry and I wanted to find a route that would get us through to the port of Bowen. Accessibility to ports is such an important thing, as Henry was to learn, painfully, later in his life.

This was in the time prior to the opening of the port of Townsville and there were two main obstacles to access: the ranges and the river, the Bowen, which stood between our properties and the port services we needed.

We had set out with just two days' rations. Seven days later we had still not found a way and we headed back to Strathmore only to find the Bowen River in full, wide flood. The current of the flooded river was formidable for anyone, let alone someone who was not a good swimmer.

We were wet, we were hungry and not just a little weary when we reached the banks of the Bowen as we had been forced to abandon our horses by this time. We had not, in fact, had anything to eat for three days so Henry's actions at that time were all the more remarkable. He decided that it would not be possible for me to cross the river, so he plunged into it and swam to the far bank. Then, as the sun went down, he walked the three miles on to Strathmore station.

I must admit I was most pleased to see him return the first thing next morning. He had brought food and a rope. Accompanying him was a member of the Native Police. With that person's help he came back across the river, fastening it to trees within the river as he went. It was only by clinging to this rope and moving from tree to tree that I was able to safely get to the opposite bank.

We were both victims of the bad times that started in the mid-1860s.

It wasn't just us, of course. The whole of Queensland was suffering. There was the drought, there was the fall of the price of wool. And there were the bank crashes.

The government itself was in strife. Those early days, after we had separated from New South Wales, there was great confidence in our new state. The government of the day was undertaking its public works on loaned money. The government's financial guarantor was the Agra and Masterman's Bank. When the bank failed, the government was in real difficulties.

MacAlister was Premier then. 'Slippery Mac' some called him because of the way he changed his mind so often. It was his grand idea – or rather his Treasurer, J.P. Bell's idea – to cope with the situation by issuing unsecured government notes. But Governor Bowen would have nothing to do with that solution. MacAlister accused the Governor of putting obstacles in the way of getting the State back onto a firm financial basis, but MacAlister resigned when Bowen stood firm. Then as unpaid men rioted in the streets of Brisbane, Robert Herbert was recalled to be Premier and find a more acceptable solution by securing loans from local and southern banks.

With MacAlister's objections ringing through the House, a dozen members left the chamber in protest. A Bill providing for bonds to the tune of £300,000 bearing interest at 10 per cent and redeemable at the end of 1869 was then rushed through the Assembly and very quickly approved by the Upper House. It was a time when public servants remained unpaid, banks were holding government cheques they could not redeem and when, thanks to the new measures introduced by Herbert, weekly amounts were being paid into government coffers to alleviate the acute financial crisis.

The combined effect of all the hardships suffered during those days then crippled many people including Henry. He lost all his properties.

Amidst all that, however, there were some happy memories. It was during those years – 1865 to be precise – that I married my Laura Theresa. It was a bad time to start a marriage, but we had some thirteen good years together before she died. Thirteen years and three children.

While I managed to remain on various properties up until '74, I decided to take up a position with the Government that year when I was appointed the warden for the Palmer goldfield. What an experience that was, caught up between 15 000 white diggers and some 20 000 Chinese.

It's interesting also to note another parallel here between myself and Henry. For it was at Cloncurry that he too, for a short period, became warden of that gold field. I know for a fact that his good common sense was put to use in resolving difficulties on that field.

Henry, however, unlike myself, was never one to seek out a public servant's life. Throughout his time in the bush, he strove to make his own individual way. He was someone who could handle deprivation, isolation and loneliness, which is why he persisted with his dream of making his life with copper. He was driven by this idea.

And he did this despite the odds. He found his wealth in many different lode discoveries. But the areas in which he made these discoveries frustrated him because of the lack of transport – getting the ore to the markets.

The lack of a railway to that region barred his ambitions.

There he was, sitting on mountains of minerals and no effective way of getting the copper to those who could process them. Remote distance – it has been such a stumbling block to many Queensland enterprises. But the railways our government talks and plans for will, I am sure, come to fruition eventually and unlock the promise this country makes to those brave, or silly enough, to penetrate the interior.

Chapter 30

A DEADLY WARNING

ALEXANDER KENNEDY

JANUARY 1884

I curse myself for not warning Henry. I could have prevented the attack that befell him that day.

The old gin had signalled to me as I was out riding through the bush. I saw her from a distance, coming out from behind a group of rocks. It almost seemed to me as if she had been hiding there. She called me to come closer. I beckoned her to come to me, away from the rocky outcrop from which she had suddenly appeared.

She came, looking around her as if she was wary of something or somebody.

'What do you want, old lady?' I asked.

She came up beside my horse, looked up at me and said, 'Henry, they gunna kill Henry.'

Who? Where? When?

But she said no more. She scurried away from me, through the broken ground and the spinifex grass. Within a minute or two she was gone. Disappearing like a whisper in the wind.

Henry was, in fact, not a great distance away. He was working his Argylla mine. He had discovered the copper lode in 1880 when he began exploring the mountain strongholds of the warrior tribe of Kalkadoons.

The Kalkadoons already had a record of attack against and the bloody murder of white settlers. Henry, however, seemed to have a knack of making friends with the wild men. Where some, including myself, would certainly keep them at arm's length, Henry was known to befriend them and even invite them into his own camp, something that was, in my opinion, akin to suicidal.

Henry's ability to get on with the blacks was so remarkable that the natives not only helped him travel through the forbidding mountains but also directed him to discovery of major copper finds there.

It was, for instance, Tubbie Terrier, himself a Kalkadoon, that guided Henry to what the miner believed to be his greatest find. Tubbie took him up into the hills via Cabbage Tree Creek and through areas that would have seemed impassable without the native as a guide. The trek into the rugged country took a number of days and, at the end of it, the last three miles of it, Tubbie told Henry the going would be too hard for horses. The party had to proceed on foot. The soles of Henry's boots were already worn through, and he was forced to trek in agony through the sharp stone and Spinifex country. The blacks in the party did the travel with ease, taking time to dash up a hillside if they caught any sight of local game such as kangaroo.

Henry stood in amazement at what he saw. His weariness disappeared as he looked up to see an outcrop of copper ore that rose to 50 feet in one spot and extended some 130 feet in an unbroken run.

Tubbie Terrier told Henry this place was called Yamamilla. Henry rephrased the name to call it Argylla.

The lode at Argylla was mainly a copper glance fixed within quartz. Part of the work required before the copper could be shipped out. This hand dressing to free the metal involved, first, the lode material being heaped and then sorted. The quartz was then separated from the ore using a hammer or some other blunt instrument. The clean marketable ore was then bagged, ready for transport.

Henry employed the local Kalkadoons to do this work. Both the men and the gins worked at the job. Ernest broke the material from the lode. The blacks sorted and bagged it. An elder of the group sat by, keeping out a rhythm of time by tapping two sticks together while the tasks were carried out with the workers chanting their own tribal songs. Henry built up this local mountain workforce to some thirty blacks and even piccaninnies were gainfully involved. In return, Henry provided the natives with an allowance of flour and corned beef.

There was no real roster to this workforce. They came and went as they pleased, sometimes electing to work and, at others, happy to go hunting in their traditional way.

At this time, Henry had with him his own 'boys', Dan and Joe, and Joe's wife Fanny, after whom Henry named one of the mountains. Throughout this period, Henry remained the only white man in the group.

Finding the Argylla lode had been an amazing achievement. Harvesting the copper from the quartz and getting it ready for shipment using the local labour was yet another accomplishment and one that few men apart from Henry would have been able to achieve. But the job was not done until Henry could get the bagged ore to a port.

It would have been a lot easier time for Henry if, by then, a rail line had pushed west to Cloncurry from the major northern port of Townsville. That link was to come, but it would be a long time in coming.

Henry elected to build a road that would enable his ore to be loaded at the Gulf port of Normanton. A road already existed between Cloncurry and Normanton and Henry decided that, with the help of the blacks, he could link Argylla to that road.

The route he chose was one starting at a tributary of the Corella River where it meets up with the Cloncurry – Normanton Road and then travelling some 36 miles into the mountains to Argylla. The first 28 miles presented little major difficulties, but the remainder of the track contained an abundance of them.

There they had to build the road between precipitous creeks and the mountain spurs above them. It meant clearing away boulders and cutting down the steep gully banks. Some days they were almost without water for either themselves or their horses. To clear the Spinifex vegetation, they burned the grass.

'It was hot, black work,' Henry told me later. 'At the end of the day you couldn't tell the difference between me and the natives. The blacks got a good chuckle out of that, I can tell you.'

'Local tribes also mistook our work for that of a hunting party. It is the local custom in this area to use fire as part of the hunting procedure. A number of times we saw distant fires that, my native workers informed me, were a response to our own blaze.'

Henry himself piloted the first teams that took ore down along the track when it was completed. The horses, he said, were straining every nerve as the whips cracked. Each wagon was loaded with four tons of copper.

'I didn't know, until we did it, whether we could claw our way out of the mountains,' Henry said. 'But, when we did, it was a source of intense satisfaction.'

It was sometime after that, when Henry had gone back to working the mine and further developing the mine that I met up with the old gin who warned me Henry's life was at risk.

I can't, for the life of me, work out why I did not go on to the mine to warn Henry.

I had, on many occasions, already warned him about the serious risks he took working among the natives.

I myself had no reason to trust them.

My first rural property posting had been at Rio on the Dawson, in the region and shortly after the time of the Cullin-la-ringo massacre. I visited that homestead while I was in the district. I saw the nineteen graves of the victims, the young men and women who the blacks had so savagely killed. It was a lesson to be learned and I learned it there and then. Take every care when dealing with the savages. Do not trust them.

That lesson was further reinforced when I moved west to Buckingham Downs, a property on Sulieman Creek in 1877. My wife, Marion, and I had been married some six years when we took up that run. With backing from the Queensland National Bank, we trekked with our cattle some 700 miles from Rockhampton to the property. We lived in a tent until the homestead was established. It was the following year that the local blacks savagely attacked and killed a man called Molvo and three other men at the Sulieman Creek waterhole. Nobody knows precisely how the attack was carried out, but it's supposed the men had gone for a swim in the waterhole and were attacked while they were defenceless.

The savages were made bold by their success and were getting ready to attack other homesteads in the district including my own, Buckingham Downs. They might well have done so, too, if it hadn't been for Sub-Inspector Edlington of the Native Police arriving to prevent such outrages. We got a group of local settlers together and with Edlington's boys we set out into the Selwyn Range where we dispersed the mobs gathered there. The Native Police went on from there, tracking the blacks down for some 70 miles and, by the time they returned, there were quite a few less blacks that local settlers needed to guard against. But the Kalkadoons, for all that, were far from beaten and still remained a real threat.

I made sure that Marion, and her sister who was married to Robert Currie, my partner on Buckingham Downs, knew how to handle firearms and how to defend themselves if there was an attack. The thought of such a move by the blacks always haunted me in those early years.

Perhaps I had become too nonchalant about the threat, and offhandedly I dismissed the message the gin had offered. It was not uncommon for natives to pass on such information – it was becoming commonplace, the utterances that this person or that person would be killed by the local natives. And the gin had offered me no real detail. No time when the threatened action would take place. Nor a place. Nor who would carry out the threat.

I know I should have taken it more seriously and gone to warn Henry. But, having done so, would Henry himself have heeded the warning? He was not one to be deterred by such talk.

Still, until this day, I blame myself for not trying to reach him.

Chapter 31

THE ATTACK

FREDERIC URQUHART
QUEENSLAND POLICE COMMISSIONER
BRISBANE, MARCH 1919

I was greatly saddened to hear of Henry's death. His life, or that part I had shared with him, held so many memories for me. It wasn't just the excitements we had shared, out there as young men on the frontier. It wasn't that we'd been figures together in the history of pioneering. Rather, I remembered the quieter times we had shared. Such as when I had been convalescing and he had brought me books, and newspapers and conversation. Like me, he had a hankering for letters and literature and there was sometimes a moment when we got to exchanging notes on stories and poems. Amongst all the adventures of those days – isn't it funny – it is the quiet times you recall, resting on the verandah in an old squatter's chair and discussing matters not remotely related to our immediate surroundings. Not that Henry was not up with the latest developments. For he was an avid reader and also a prolific letter writer.

But it's funny, too, that Henry should die this way. In peace and far from the from the frontier. For here was a man who had faced death so often that you would think they had become old friends.

There was no chance of drowning the man. The number of flooded creeks and rivers he'd swum were too many to count. There was the time when fever nearly overtook him up in the Gulf country. But he beat that too. He had had horses fall on him; he'd confronted murderous mobs on the 'Curry goldfields. He'd had spears thrown at him more than once. And he had been plunged into poverty from a heady plane of wealth, something which broke many others. But not Henry.

I don't know if Henry feared death. I know it was never his greatest fear. His greatest fear, I am sure, was one of failure. His dream was of success, no matter what it took and how long it took. Death did not seem to feature largely in his thoughts. Not that he was foolhardy. But he took risks that many others would not. Like going into Kalkadoon territory virtually alone in search of his goal – copper.

If ever he should have died, it was in that attack of '84. It was just before I got there but I got to know the details later, partly from Alexander Kennedy and also from Henry himself.

He was out at his Argylla mine. The irony of Henry's life, undoubtedly, was that he succeeded in finding such rich lodes but had no way of capitalising on those finds. Argylla was a good example of this. There was no way he could exploit that field if he couldn't get the copper to a port. In those days, and for many years later, there was no railroad to Cloncurry. So, Henry had made his own, a road from the Cloncurry – Burketown track which connected to the mine.

With the help of local blacks, he had blazed and broken that track into the mountainous wilderness. Without the help of the natives – the Kalkadoons, in fact – Henry would not have been able to work that mine which was in their territory. You have to keep in mind that this was a time when these same blacks were menacing everyone else. Cloncurry itself was in fear of its very existence, fearing an attack from the nearby savages. The situation is even more peculiar because Henry, in recent years, had been associated with Kennedy, helping Kennedy locate new runs for his cattle. As anyone in the far northwest knew, Kennedy was a sworn foe to the Kalkadoons.

From what he later told me, I know that Henry had made it his business to keep on good terms with the blacks.

'For the last two years, at least,' he told me, 'I have frequently had the blacks with me, and I have always acted the same towards them. I have made presents to them. If they are willing to work for me, I have also fed them.'

'I have always been on the best of terms with them,' he stated.

Which was why he was not just wounded in the attack but, also, stunned by how it happened.

Henry, on that January day, was bridling his horse. He intended travelling to Cloncurry to get more supplies to keep the mine working.

He was aware that some of the blacks he had with him were unhappy about all the hard work that they had undertaken in recent weeks. It was back-breaking labour, clearing the roadway, shifting boulders out of the path, breaking down creek banks to enable easy crossings of creek beds. He had heard a few irritable remarks from some of the natives. One native, in particular, was sowing dissent among the mob. So, Henry had confronted him earlier that day, telling him that if he wasn't prepared to do the work, he could go without his corned beef and damper breakfast.

'If that's what you think, go and get your own tucker from the bush,' Henry had told the Aboriginal.

When the attack came, it was from behind. Henry was fitting the bridle to his horse when, according to Henry, 'A blackfellow drove a spear into my back. I turned around to find him closing on me.'

The black had picked the moment for his attack. Henry's two Mitakoodi blackboys, Dan and Joe, were not in camp. They were away chasing horses that had wandered during the previous night. And Henry was unarmed. In fact, his guns, I'm told, had been removed from the camp.

So, Henry was unarmed and without an ally, the others there being kinsmen of the attacker. The native had picked up the spear and driven it into Henry's back. Here at least, Henry had some slight luck. The spear struck him below the shoulder and also hit bone which saved him from the spear going any further.

Despite the dizziness and the blood flowing from him, Henry met the other's advance. Part of the spear broke away but his fight for his life continued with some of the spear still embedded.

The black grabbed Henry by the throat but Henry broke the grip and in turn attempted to strangle the attacker. They rolled to the ground where the blackfellow tried to get his hands onto a rock which would have smashed Henry's skull.

The fiend called on his tribesmen to help him. But none did. Through the fury of all this turmoil, they stood back impassively watching the desperate struggle between the two. Joe's wife, Fanny, and several of the bush gins, however, were shrieking in agitation. They ran hither and thither with piteous cries but would not come anywhere near the two wrapped in mortal combat.

The blackfellow wore little and the only real grip Henry could get was on the man's hair. But the native, realising that – even wounded – Henry was not going to be overcome, eventually broke free and ran off into the bush.

Henry, a tall sinewy man, had his tough life to thank. The hardships he faced on a daily basis and his vigorous adherence to rigorous manual labour gave him the ability to overcome his grievous wound and free himself from his cowardly attacker. The man had, undoubtedly, been counting on the support of the twenty fighting men who were in camp that day.

Henry staggered to his grass hut a short distance away. There he was to lay for two days on his blankets and never moved. He felt, he later recalled, as if he had been stuffed with a ramrod. He had lost considerable blood. The wound had also partially paralysed him. The head of the spear remained lodged in his body.

The other blacks, now that the fight had finished, did what they could for Henry.

'I made them put flannel shirts round my body and kept soaking them with hot water for three days and three nights,' Henry later recorded. 'On the third day I got great relief and was able to lie outside during the day.'

Shortly after Henry had made it to his hut, his blackboys, Joe and Dan, had returned to camp from their chase after the horses.

'I despatched the two to the nearest station, Fort Constantine, which was some 40 miles away,' Henry had told me. 'It was my earnest hope they could find someone there to come to my rescue.'

The two Mitakoodis decided that they would travel faster on foot. The distance they had to cover was broken by stony ravines and turpentine thickets that horses could not traverse. In readiness,

Joe and Dan removed their European clothes and, armed only with a tomahawk stuck in their belts and a handful of their own native weapons, they took off into the ranges towards the station.

Back in the camp, Henry waited in agony. He was unable to see the wound in his back and nor could he touch it. However, he had some oatmeal in his stores. He had been using this for making porridge. Now he had Fanny and some of the other gins make the oatmeal into poultices which, when applied to the wound, kept inflammation away.

But the wound was just part of Henry's worries. While he remained prone and defenceless within the hut, the other blacks assembled at the camp.

'They were quarrelling every night,' Henry said. 'I have not the slightest doubt that they were disputing as to whether they should kill me or not, no doubt, fearing I should send the police after them.'

Three days after they had set out for Fort Constantine, Joe and Dan returned to the Argylla camp. They had covered more than 80 miles on foot in the three days. But, for Henry, their report was devastating.

Roger Sheaffe, Henry's long-time friend who owned the station, was away when Joe and Dan reached Fort Constantine. The stockriders were also away from the station homestead. The only person there was a hut keeper – a grey bearded old Norwegian sailor. He was, to say the least, most suspicious about two naked, armed natives. And, in any case, he could not understand what they were trying to tell him.

Five days after the attack, Henry calculated that the natives had decided not to kill him where he lay. But no one was coming to rescue him, and he would still die unless he tried to get back to the town. That meant riding some 60 miles back to Cloncurry though the wilderness of mountains and watercourses and in the blazing heat of summer. A parched summer that had not yet brought any rains to feed the creeks and rivers.

He told Dan and Joe of his plans. The Mitakoodis saddled his horse and their own and brought provisions including water. What would happen when he, with the help of his blackboys, mounted his horse? The pain was acute as he rose into the saddle and slumped over the front of it. Dan and Joe rode on either side, helping him to stay upright. But Henry could see some dozen men standing in the path they intended to take. The two blackboys walked the horses towards the men who, as they came up to them, parted to make way for the small party. When the trio rode through, some of the warriors chased after them. Not to halt them but to accompany Henry, Joe and Dan.

That day the party, constrained by countryside and Henry's distress, made just 10 miles. It was here that the Kalkadoon blacks left and went back to their mountains. Still in agony, Henry, together with the Mitakoodis, pushed on the next day to cover a little more than the first day's travel.

By now Henry could travel no further and needed to rest. This he did to recover his strength. That allowed him to ride some 15 miles on the fourth day of the trek.

But by now they were running out of water and Cloncurry was still some 25 miles to go. The three pushed on and, despite finding no water along the way, they reached their goal late that day. They had made it and Henry was soon receiving the medical treatment he so badly needed.

Chapter 32

WAITING

Ernest Henry, Cloncurry 1886

Success is dearer to me than the possession of wealth. I've dreamed of both, and both have mainly, till now, eluded me. But I shall have success, I'm certain, in seeing my dreams come true and hopefully the wealth will still pass to my children.

I don't want you to think I am cavilling over my own good or bad fortune – far from it. I've had dreams of what could be. I've been blessed – with the best parents a chap could have – with a robust health that has seen me through much, and a land full of promise and there for the hard work.

But it has been close-on thirty years now since I first arrived from home. My father, who gave me such support in my endeavours, died before I ever saw him again. I was able to see my aging mother recently when I returned home to England on business. She, like him, continues to support my promise if not any great material success. May God continue to bless her with good health.

I am proud to call myself a pioneer.

For those past thirty years I have struggled in the foremost ranks against the misfortunes which have invariably attended the early pioneers of Northern Queensland.

I have no wish for, and have never sought, any recognition for anything I have done towards the occupation of the northern territory of Queensland. But I believe few, if any, have practically done more.

I take no credit. I work for myself and those belonging to me, but I do expect the fruits of my labour.

So much has happened since I first arrived. So much has changed.

Nearly all the pioneers of the far north have met with misfortune. I was the first to lead the way with stock, over to the Gulf waters, and of my then contemporaries, few, very few, remain in the ranks. Very many are dead – numbers 'threw up the sponge' and retreated southward, their places being filled by those who came after all risks and difficulties had been overcome by their predecessors at the cost, in most instances, of their all.

Pioneering here, beyond the limits of civilisation, is like a forlorn hope. A host stride over the fallen and reap the rewards of the fight.

It is hardly encouraging to those who incur all the risks in opening the way to future wealth of the Colony to find themselves but steppingstones for others, for many who have never known the need to work a single day.

Chapter 33

HENRY'S LETTER TO HIS MOTHER

CLONCURRY

28 JANUARY 1884

My Dear Mother,

I returned to Cloncurry a few days ago in a rather sorry plight. Do not be alarmed, for I am nearly well now, and don't alarm yourself for the future for I promise to take more care of myself. The fact is, I have been speared by a blackfellow. It happened at my new copper mine, Argylla. I had been employing several natives to help me in clearing a track between Cloncurry and Argylla. On the 15th instant I was saddling my horses intending to return here. When in the act of bridling a horse, a blackfellow drove a spear into my back, who, on my turning round, immediately closed with me. I was unarmed at the time and, being partially paralysed by the wound and exhausted by the loss of blood, I had a desperate struggle before I could free myself from the brute. As soon as I cast him off, he decamped. When I was first speared, I was sure they were all against me, and I was doomed. But although the fiend yelled to the others to help him, not one would move to his assistance, though there were over twenty fighting men in the camp. At first, I had no hope of recovering, for I thought the spear had broken in me, and felt as if I was stuffed with a rod of iron. I have a small hut at Argylla made of grass, and in it I lay down on my blankets, and for two days and nights never moved. The other blacks watched and did all they could for me. I made them put flannel shirts round my body and kept soaking them with hot water for three days and nights. On the third day I got great relief and was able to lie outside during the day. At first, I suffered agony. Immediately after it happened, I started two boys to the nearest station, distant about 40 miles, for help. They returned the third day saying there was no one at home, but as I was feeling better, I did not mind so much, though it was rather an anxious time, for my other blacks had assembled at the camp, and were quarrelling every night. I have not the slightest doubt but that they were disputing as to whether they should kill me or not, no doubt, fearing I should send the police after them. However, all went well, and on the fifth day I managed to ride about 10 miles on my way here, several blacks going with me. Second day, I made about the same distance and rested the next. The following day rode 15 miles, and the fifth and last day I had to make 23 miles as there was no water on the way and arrived at Cloncurry rather exhausted as you may well imagine, but otherwise mending fast.

The only reason I can assign for the assault on me is that I had stopped the man's rations, because he would not work, and several others the same way, and it is a most extraordinary thing that none of them would help him.

For the last two years or more, I have frequently had the blacks with me, and have always acted the same towards them, making presents to and feeding those who worked for me and have always been on the best of terms with them. I know you will be anxious about me, and so will promise you not to go out again alone. I must tell you, or you will think my recovery marvellous, that on the way to Cloncurry I kept applying to my back oatmeal poultices. They seemed to have a most beneficial effect and kept inflammation away.

Believe me, my dear Mother
Ever you affec. son
Ernest Henry

Bibliography

Notes from *Discovery Cloncurry* Cloncurry Historical Society, 2002.

Kenyon, Justine, *Aboriginal Words from Aboriginal Word Book*, Lothian Publishing Co. Pty Ltd, Melbourne, 1951.

Robinson, J.S. *Arms in the Service of Queensland:* 1859 -1901, National Library of Australia, 1997.

Australian Dictionary of Biography. Details on. Frederic Urquhart, Augustus Frederick Elphinstone, Alexander Kennedy, Philip Frederic Sellheim.

Grassby, Al, Mark Hill, *The Battle of Battle Mountain, Six Australian Battlefields* By Al Grassby and Marki Hill Angus & Robertson Publishers 1988, Copyright © Al Grassby and Marji Hill 1988.

Urquhart's Report on Mountain Battle, Native Police, QSA A/41765, Stamped received by -Inspector of Police Muttaburra 14285 and Commissioner of Police Queensland 2369 I Wing April 8 1885 N.M. Police Office, Cloncurry, March 8th 1885.

Births, Deaths and Marriages Registry ... Ernest Henry, Marian Elizabeth Henry (nee Thompson) and their children.

Kennedy, Edward B and John Murray, Black Police of Queensland,

Reminiscences of official work and personal adventures in the early days of the colony, Albemarle Street, London 1902.

Laurie, Arthur, The Black Wars, *The Black War in Queensland*, Royal Historical Society of Queensland, Special Journal to mark the Centenary of Queensland 1859 – 1959, 6, 1 1959, (Read before the Meeting of the Royal Historical Society of Queensland on October 23, 1958)

Palmer, Edward, *Early Days in North Queensland*, Angus and Robertson, Sydney, 1903.

Gray, Robert, *Reminiscences of India and North Queensland* 1857 – 1912. London: Constable, 1913.

Sir George Ferguson Bowen 1821 – 1899. *Thirty Years of Colonial Government Vol I,* Mullen's Library, 29 & 31 Collins Street East, Melbourne. Single Subscription, One guinea per annum. *Letter to the Editor, (pasted within the front cover of this book) by G.F.Bown and dated August 20ᵗʰ 1898: Respecting Queensland and other Australasian Colonies.*

Sir George Ferguson Bowen: Letter to Colonial Secretary re. Dalrymple expedition. Queensland State Archives, item 17670, page 203, letter number 34.

Urquhart, Frederic Camp Canzonettes, Notes by Frederic Urquhart, Gordon & Gotch, 1891, re. the poems he wrote.

Boulton, G.C., A Thousand Miles Away: a history of North Queensland Australian National University Press 1970. Re. Robert Christison of Lammermoor.

Holthouse, Hector Cloncurry Discovery Brief, <u>Source: *Illustrated History of Queensland*</u>, Rigby 1978 p.185.

Baird, David Walkabout Magazine article April 1969: (re. Cloncurry history)

Rowley C.D. *The Destruction of Aboriginal Society*, A series sponsored by The Social Science Research Council of Australia, Australian National University Press, 1971.

Pike, Grenville, *Queensland Frontier,-* Rigby Limited, Brisbane 1978.

Henry, Ernestine M, Ernest Henry's Family Particulars supplied by his daughter Miss Ernestine M. Henry.

Source: Ernest Henry Papers 1863- 1919, Ref No OM90 -18 Box No 9205, John Oxley Library.

Henry, Ernest, Hughenden: *An Account by Ernest Henry of an Exploration Trip Resulting in the Taking Up of Hughenden Station.* Source: Ernest Henry Papers 1863- 1919, Ref No OM90 -18, Box No 9205.John Oxley Library. Tuesday, 24th November, 1863.

Badly deteriorated letter (by Urquhart) re reasons for wishing to join police force: Sent to General Fielding, then resident in Queensland.

Personal and professional details of Frederic Urquhart: The Historical Society of Queensland Journal, Volume 4.

HENRY RECORDS JAMES COOK UNIVERSITY

Extracts from early letters of Ernest Henry (manuscript) by Henry, Ernest. Subjects:

Henry, Ernest. Correspondence

Queensland – History – 1824-1900 – sources

Call numbers 994 37031 v 1,2,3 and 4

N.Q. Descriptors: Dawson River, Boroondah, Henry, Ernest , Burdekin River, Pioneers, Pastoral Industry, History.

Call number 994.37031 HEN T 5

N.Q. descriptors: Henry, Ernest ... Hughenden Station, Explorations, Flinders River, Aborigines, Aboriginal Hostilities, Sutton River.

Call number 994 37032 HEN T 4

Henry, Ernest – Diaries –Cloncurry – Copper Mining- Geological exploration = Sweers Island – Landsborough, W William – Aborigines

Call number 994 37032 HEN T 2

Call number 994 37032 HEN T 6

Call number 994 37032 HEN T 7

Call number 994 37032 HEN T 3

Diary and field notes 994 37041 HEN T 3

An account of Ernest Henry of an exploring trip resulting in the taking up of Hughenden Station 994.37051 HEN T 5

Account of exploration: including the first discovery of copper at Cloncurry 994.37041.HEN T 4

Portion of diary dated 10 March through to 31 October 1867 by Ernest HENRY 994.37041 HEN T 7

Call number 994 3092 HEN/PHI ... the discoverer and principal prospector of the Cloncurry mineral district of North-West Queensland by Phillips, George

Readings in North Queensland mining history edited by H.K. Kennedy, published by Townsville: History Department James Cook University of North Queensland 1980-82. Call number J338.2099436

STATE LIBRARY OF QUEENSLAND

OM90-18 Ernest Henry papers 1863-1919

QUEENSLAND STATE ARCHIVES

Native Mounted Police records

Police Reports: Sergeant M.G. Green, Cloncurry, to Inspector Lamond, Normanton, 8 June 1899 POL 14B/15, 58

Votes and Proceedings Legislative Assembly, Queensland 1861:Report from the Select Committee on the Native Police Force and the condition of the Aborigines generally.

Inquest into the Death of Marcus de La Poer Beresford who was murdered on the night of the 24th January by the blacks about 20 miles from the Farley Head Station in the MacKinlay Ranges, Queensland State Archives file: JUS N91 59/1883 Z3437Date Marked: Crown Law Office 2nd March 1883 Farley January 28th 1883. Magisterial Inquiry before A.A Hart J.P.

Alexander Kennedy and QANTAS: Sydney Bulletin, 1971.

Blainey, Geffery, *Mines in the Spinifex*. Angus and Robertson, Halstead Press, Sydney 1960.

Notes on the Political History of Queensland 1859 -1917 By Charles A Bernays, Clerk-Assistant and Sergeant-at-Arms, Legislative Assembly. *The Historical Society of Queensland Journal Vol. 1 January 1918 No 4.*

Pearson S.E., The Prospector of Argylla, being an account of the Life of the late E. Henry To his daughter Ernestine Marian Henry, daughter of Ernest Henry

John Oxley Library- OM74-8 1930.

Reynolds, Henry, *The Other Side of the Frontier.* Penguin Books – 1995

Fysh, Hudson, *Taming the North*, Angus and Robertson, Sydney1950: First published 1933 [Location: John Oxley Library]

Hardy, Perry, *The Cloncurry Story*, from: John Oxley Library Q. 994.37 HAR C2

Lack, Clem, Harry Stafford, *The Rifle and the Spear*, Fortitude Press, Brisbane 1964.

Armstrong, Robert E.M. *The Kalkadoons*, William Brooks & Co Pty Ltd Brisbane 1979.

D'arcy Uhr: Wikipedia.org

Urquhart's report on the Murder of J.W. Powell of Calton Hills *(marked –received by Commissioner of Police Queensland October 2,1884) (addressed initially to Sub Inspector Ahern, Muttaburra)* N. M. Police Office Cloncurry. August 21st 1884.

URQUHART RECORDS Urquhart, Fredric Charles (1858 – 1935) Published in Australian Dictionary of Biography Volume 12 (MUP) 1990

Black Police, The Black Police of Queensland, *Reminiscences of Official Work and Personal Adventures in The Early days of the Colony.*, By Edward B. Kennedy, London, John Murray, Albemarle Street 1902.

Queensland State Archives, Digital Images, D R 5644 (Item ID it's 17670)

9 781925 707847